A Deathly Shade of Passion

A Clairemont Island Mystery Series

by

Vicki Williams

Copyright © 2020 Vicki Williams

First published in 2020

Printed Ingram Spark/Lightning Source

1st Edition 1 September 2020

ISBN: 978-0-9876306-6-7 Paperback

ISBN: 978-0-9876306-7-4 eBook

ISBN: 978-0-9876306-8-1 Hardcover

Published: Red Eagle Publications

Editing: Firebird Consulting Editing

Cover Design: GermanCreative

vickiwilliamsauthor.com.au

Dedication

This book is dedicated to the many people who continue to support and encourage me, especially over the twenty-two months it took me to write *A Deathly Shade of Passion*.

To those of you, who read, edited my drafts gave me valuable feedback and encouraged me to lose myself in imagination, I give thanks.

A very special thank you to my family and friends, you have always believed in me, and support all my writing projects. Your loving support and encouragement are welcomed with open arms regardless of the distance.

CHAPTER ONE

Eye Spy

The ferry crossing to Sydney went without a hitch. Oliver Smith went about his usual routine, the same he did for every other crossing. He loved the job, and got on really well with the rest of the crew aboard the Clairemont ferry. Jerry had now retired, but Oliver thanked him for taking a punt on him all those years ago.

Normally he'd sit on deck to enjoy his break, but today, even though the sun was shining bright in the cloudless blue sky, he had a chill running the length of his spine. He had no idea why he was chilled—there was virtually no wind—so he opted to sit on a solitary deckchair hidden behind rows of cars, away from the prying eyes of passengers. As he rolled a joint, he remembered how he came to get this job.

It was thirty years ago when a young twenty-year-old Oliver, beaten to within an inch of his life, landed in Sydney, trying to change his appearance. Alas, there was nothing he could do to obscure the deep knife wound that ran from the corner of his left eye, all the way down to his jawline. This would be a constant reminder of his sins. Every time he looked in the mirror he was taken back to his youth, a time he would dearly love to forget.

As a young man in a new city, Oliver roamed the Sydney streets looking for work. Eventually the chatter around him grew more intense, as did the smell of the ocean, and he realized he had found his way to a port area. Fishing nets hung outside windows to dry, the pavement turned to cobblestones; the rows of cafeterias offering outdoor seating under large umbrellas far outweighed other shopping options. The smell of food and coffee became overpowering: it was then he realised how hungry he was. He stopped at one of the cafés to peruse the menu, a great selection at affordable prices. He looked inside and was pleasantly surprised with the décor. The café was reasonably packed, with music playing softly in the background.

The older gentleman seated next to him was reading the paper, strong looking, but not muscular like a body builder. With a receding hairline and toothless grin, this guy was visually quite a character. Oliver wondered what he did for a living; he guessed it was something outdoors as the sleeveless shirt revealed an obvious tan line. He wore cargo shorts and runners. Sensing someone was watching him; he looked up and caught sight of Oliver.

"Something I can help you with, mate?" the stranger asked.

"Sorry. I was just trying to read the paper, that's all," Oliver replied, hoping his response would suffice.

"Here, why don't you read it while I eat my breakfast?"

"Thanks. That would be great. I actually want to check for jobs," Oliver stated.

As the stranger handed over the paper, he asked what kind of work Oliver was looking for.

"Anything really, I've just arrived from New Zealand so

I'm willing to try anything that doesn't require a qualification or expertise. I've done mainly seasonal work. I'm a hard worker and gained loads of skills, but unfortunately I haven't gained a qualification in anything."

"Tell me more about where you've worked, I'm interested to hear the kinds of things you've done and what skills those jobs have taught you. By the way, my name is Jerry."

The two shook hands as Oliver introduced himself. He then spent the next hour explaining the seasonal work he'd done in New Zealand, omitting his most recent job, no point in mentioning that kind of work if he wanted a job in Sydney.

Jerry asked about the scar. Oliver ran his finger down the length of it, still tender and sore to touch; he ashamedly blamed it on his father, stating that that was the reason he left New Zealand. There was no way he was going to divulge the real reason.

"Oliver, were you serious about trying anything?"

"Yeah. Why?"

"I manage a crew aboard a ferry that runs Sydney to Clairemont Island. I'm looking for a new guy to help out on deck. Doing mooring and anchoring duties, cargo operations and some engine room maintenance. Is this something you may be interested in doing?" Jerry asked.

"I don't have any experience on ships. Hell, I've never even been on a boat before. Are you sure you want to offer me a job?" Oliver was quite taken by the offer, wondering what the catch was.

"Yes, I'm serious, I've just listened to you talk about where you've worked. The passion, dedication you had for the work is evident. The respect and loyalty for your bosses and co-workers speaks volumes. Seems I have gained quite an insight into you and, yes, I'm pretty sure I would like to offer you the job. It doesn't pay much to start with and the hours are long, but for a single guy like yourself I'm sure you'll enjoy the lifestyle. What do you reckon, want to give it a try? Think about it for a few minutes while I finish my breakfast."

Oliver did just that, it took him two seconds to make a decision. For him it was a no brainer. It was a job. Done and dusted.

"When do I start?" Oliver asked.

"Tomorrow, if you like. I can take you down to the office when we've finished breakfast to fill in the paperwork. The ferry runs seven days with four return crossings each day, although you will only do one return crossing daily. You will work twelve-hour shifts: four on, three off. It may sound like a long day, but to be honest it's pretty easy, with loads of downtime once your work's complete and the passengers are settled into their crossing."

"Lead the way," Oliver said, as he acknowledged the new start of his life.

Heaven forbid, Oliver thought, where have those thirty years gone? So much has happened since that day, and to be honest he wouldn't change any of it. With his morning tea break over, it was time to get back to work and prepare for docking in Sydney. He'd had a busy week and desperately needed to replenish his stock.

As Oliver moved his fifty-year-old body deftly through the familiar route to his destination he was mindful of the time. He took advantage of this shift as it allowed him just enough time to reach his destination and get back to the dock in time to make last minute preparations for the return trip to Clairemont Island. He had a standard order and usually his supplier was waiting for him at a quiet cafe, but today he wasn't there when Oliver arrived. Oliver had fifteen minutes up his sleeve, so he grabbed the cafe's complimentary newspaper and proceeded to flick through it as he drank his coffee.

It was as he glanced toward the headline on the right hand

page that Oliver's eyes rose from the paper and onto the face of his old friend, Hōne, a friend he'd gone to school in New Zealand with, worked with and one of the two friends that saved his life. But, for all intents and purposes, Oliver was supposed to be dead; therefore it was essential that Oliver pull the newspaper up over his face in an effort to conceal his identity. Just as Oliver's supplier sat down opposite him, he noticed Hōne had sat at a table on the other side of the cafe; he was facing in Oliver's direction. Oliver hoped and prayed he was far enough away so as not to be noticed as he continued to transact his business. Five minutes later, Oliver exited the cafe as inconspicuously as possible and returned directly to the ferry where he boarded and immediately set about doing his required duties for the return trip to Clairemont Island.

He didn't give Hōne another thought until he was well out to sea, when he was on his afternoon tea break. He stood on deck with the wind lashing his face as Sydney disappeared into the distance. Hōne and Oliver had been friends ever since Oliver found out he was adopted.

It seemed an eon ago when Oliver's mother told him the shocking news. He was only ten years old, and he remembered the shocked relief he felt at the time. Shock because it came out of the blue. Relief because when, after another of his father's ranting alcoholic tirades, as he sat watching his beaten mother sob uncontrollably, he asked why she never fought back, why she didn't leave him. Her feeble voice asserted she didn't have the strength and where would she go, she didn't have any money or friends to support her. This was her lot in life and she had to accept it.

When Oliver was younger he used to cradle her in his arms and hold her until her tears subsided. She noticed over the years that he stopped trying to console her. She realised he didn't even pity her anymore and that his nurturing feeling had turned to anger, anger at her for allowing herself to be his punching bag and anger at his father for being a bastard. Many a time, he had stated he was going to kill his father for what he put them all through and, as he grew up, she sensed he might be capable of actually doing it.

Identifying that time might be running out, she knew if she didn't tell him the truth, he might never know his true identity. With tears in her eyes she gently explained that they adopted him when he was five days old. As she rifled through the filing cabinet in an effort to source his birth certificate, he glanced over to the person he called his father. Then it clicked. That feeling he had always carried around, that feeling of not belonging. Oliver had now worked out why he loathed that drunken good for nothing lowlife passed out on the sofa. He was not his biological father. Thank god for that, he mused.

His mother handed him his birth certificate. As clear as day, stated in black and white, were the names of his birth mother and father. With a smile on his face, he read and reread that certificate. Over and over he read the words until he knew it by heart.

He looked into the eyes of the woman who brought him up, the person he called his mother. As waves of emotion flooded his system, he had no idea how to react. He was torn between anger and gratefulness. Anger that it took till now to tell him he was adopted, and grateful that these two people were not his parents. Maybe now his life would change for the better. Well, that was what he thought, as a young and innocent ten-year-old.

Retreating to his bedroom to digest what had just unfolded, Oliver pondered his next move. He loathed his parents, that was a given. But how did he feel about his birth mother and father? He wasn't sure if they deserved his anger or envy.

Suddenly he was flooded with questions. Why did they give him up? Where were they now? Would they want to meet him? Would they love him, want him, care for him? How could he find them? Every question raised half a dozen other questions. He played devil's advocate, trying to answer them in a way that gave him what he wanted. A life that was better than the one he was living. If truth be known, he secretly wanted his birth mother to save him, save him from this life, the life he'd lived for ten years. After all, it was her fault he was here in this hellhole. She owed him—big time.

The next few years were lost in a world of turmoil and joy. The highlight for him was when his father was killed as he staggered home from the pub one cold winter's night. He was struck and killed instantly by a drink driver. It's ironic how one can take the life of another.

This was a roller coaster ride of hell for Oliver: in one moment he was full of sorrow and the next he was filled with levels of happiness, then guilt. He spent less and less time at home, the sight of his mother depressed him. He felt nothing for her now; he blamed her for the life she led. He blamed her for what he had been put through, and the life he was forced to live.

For some reason, he failed to or didn't realise that he hardly ever blamed his father for what was dealt at the mercy of his hands. It wasn't as though he idolised his father; it was more that Oliver didn't know how to compartmentalise his feelings and emotions for his father, other than to call him a worthless, useless waste of space.

The birth certificate stated his birth mother had a Maori surname. Oliver had never had anything to do with the Maori way of life. A white Pakeha and loner, he didn't know anything about Maori ancestry. There were a few Maori boys at his school; he decided to ask them what he should know about being a Maori. One day he would meet his mother and he didn't want to embarrass himself by being an ignorant Pakeha.

Two Maori boys were in his English class, during lunch break the next day Oliver nervously approached them, asking awkwardly what they had done over the weekend; as a result a friendship was formed.

The antics of most teenage boys are something you put up with depending, on the severity of the deed, but Hōne and Joe were different. They raised high stakes, the deed was extreme, but the pay-off was exhilarating. Oliver was hooked; he had found friends that 'got him', respected him and would do anything for him. With these boys, he had found friendship.

The years that followed saw him leave school at fifteen. Together with Hōne and Joe he travelled the South Island of New Zealand doing seasonal work. He didn't visit his mother to say goodbye, to let her know of his plans. There was no point telling her where he was headed. She was no longer his family, he had distanced himself from her long before, she was not part of his life anymore; in truth she was dead to him. It was as if, unknowingly, she had served her purpose.

His favourite job was working in the shearing sheds as a roustabout, where he would sweep the floors, grade and bale the fleece. The shearers and other roustabouts were a great bunch of guys; they worked really hard seven days a week at each shed, but in-between sheds and when it rained they had time off where they would let their hair down, go feral, get drunk and screw eager young women. They made heaps of money, but spent it just as quickly.

It was quite by chance they met Matt, another young Maori. Matt asked if they would like to make some extra money. They unanimously agreed and were introduced to his family, a notorious bikie gang. Oliver had heard of the gang, even though he wasn't exactly sure what they did. Matt assured them they would be well looked after and treated as part of the family, and that was all Oliver needed to hear, he was ready and willing to do anything to become one with family, any family other than the screwed up one he had grown up in.

Matt was true to his word: it didn't take long before Oliver felt as if he was part of an extended family. If he could change the colour of his skin he would. But the fact that he was a Pakeha never got in the way of how he felt. He was a Maori through and through. After all, he was born a white Maori, wasn't he?

The following years were a blur; he worked hard and without question he did anything the family asked of him. He started committing petty crimes at first. The hardest was his first burglary; he remembered it as though it was yesterday. The thrill of breaking into someone's home as they slept, making his way through the rooms, grabbing the goods and then escaping without getting caught. The adrenalin rush was better than any drug he could get his hands on. The euphoric state afterward was beyond belief. He was hooked. Under the watchful eye of the family he became a valuable commodity.

He married young, which was a mistake on so many levels. Against the wishes of the gang, Oliver married Zeta, the eldest daughter of Tiny, the chapter president.

His warped idea of what a family should be was hindered by his upbringing. The thoughts of his parents pained him as he tried desperately to obliterate them from his mind. He didn't want to think of them. He didn't want to model his married life on them. He had hated every minute of his childhood and vowed he'd never represent their model of husband and wife. In saying that, he didn't know how else to act or behave.

Needless to say, he struggled from day one. Being married was not easy and being a loving husband was even worse.

Not being able to reciprocate love, affection or communication, he eventually found other ways to meet his needs. In the beginning that came in the form of a bottle, later on he developed a taste for young and innocent women.

In an effort to keep his indiscretions quiet, Oliver began spending less and less time around the gang. Tiny suspected things at home were not satisfactory. Zeta was forever going on and on about how Oliver was never around, and when he was there, he was always exhausted. Knowing exactly how much work Oliver was doing for the gang, Tiny became curious as to what Oliver was doing with his spare time.

In just a few weeks of tailing Oliver, Tiny had everything he needed to regretfully make the next move. After calling an extraordinary meeting, Tiny, the chapter president, announced Oliver's fateful outcome. He was to be taught a lesson—gang style.

Matt, who had introduced Oliver to the family, was handed the unfortunate task. He in turn appointed Joe and Hōne to do the deed. Oliver's lifelong friends were none too happy with the prospect of doing him in, but to stay loyal to the family they knew their future was at stake: if they didn't do what they were told, then they too would be dealt a fatal blow.

Tiny informed Joe and Hōne where they would find Oliver. At two on a Tuesday morning they busted him in a hotel room bed where he lay between two beautiful young women. With a gun pointed at Oliver's forehead all Hōne muttered was: "Tiny told us where to find you." There was nothing more to be said; Oliver knew his number was up.

Acting on impulse Oliver jumped out of bed as both Joe and Hōne lashed at him fists hitting their target. As Oliver fought with Joe he was unaware that Hōne had pulled a knife from the concealed compartment in his boot. Hōne had no intention of doing permanent damage to Oliver, they were mates. Struggling with indecision Hōne waited for Joe to take a breather, it was then he stepped forward, closer than he'd intended. The knife found its target, Hōne realised what he'd done, quickly he pulled the knife down out of the way, but the damage was evident. A deep gash had left its mark on Oliver, down the length of his face, from the corner of his eye to his jawline. Blood spewed from the open wound.

Realising there was no point in doing any more harm to each other, they conceded defeat. Hōne held a towel over the wound to stop the bleeding as he made it abundantly clear that Oliver understood the situation he'd put them in. With deep regret they handed Oliver a fake passport, gave him a wad of cash and told him never to return to New Zealand, to go somewhere he would never be found, and that's just what he did.

At least, until today, he had gone under the radar, he hoped and prayed that Hōne had not recognised him at the cafe. All the way back to the ferry, Oliver had kept glancing over his shoulder to make sure he wasn't followed and he didn't think he was, but the queasy feeling in the pit of his stomach wasn't going away.

Hōne had certainly noticed Oliver in the cafe, he'd have recognised him anywhere, he remembered the night he put the scar down the length of his face, following orders. He wondered if Oliver blamed him for what they'd done to him that night. As Hōne followed Oliver down the narrow laneways that led to the port, Hōne was careful not to be seen, but after the second close call he decided to call in a third party. He approached a middle aged European gentleman seated on a park bench. He asked if he'd like to earn some extra cash for following Oliver and obtaining as much intel as he could about him. The European agreed, was given a wad of cash with the promise of more. The description of Oliver was pretty spot on as he followed him aboard the ferry to Clairemont Island.

As Hōne waited for the phone call, he paced the length of his hotel room, wondering what he'd do once he received the information.

He really wanted to walk up to Oliver in the cafe, to catch up, find out what Oliver had been up to over the last thirty years. He wanted to tell Oliver that Joe had passed away in prison. Guilt had slowly killed Joe; he'd never recovered from defying Tiny that night. The longer he worked in the gang the more guilt-ridden he became, until he eventually stopped caring, it was then he made stupid mistakes that cost the gang dearly. Taking the heat off Hōne, Joe took the fall for his mate with a death sentence, which came sooner than expected.

Hōne's loyalty now lay with Tiny and the gang. Deep in his heart he knew he had to tell Tiny of the deception all those years ago. He also knew there was a good chance his days would be numbered, as opposed to just being outcast from the gang.

When the ferry docked at Clairemont Island, Oliver watched every passenger get off. Thankfully Hōne was not on board, and Oliver eventually relaxed enough to walk home in peace. He did not notice the stranger who was paid to watch his every move on the ferry and follow him to his home.

The middle aged European man was feeling pretty pleased with himself. The thousand dollars burning a hole in his pocket was nothing compared to the other four thousand coming his way upon confirmed address details. Thoughts of how this money would change his life filled his mind as he dialed the mobile number of the Maori man in Sydney.

CHAPTER TWO

Troy Pops the Question

Cautiously optimistic, Troy Anderson opened his legal practice on Clairemont Island. He hired a law student and legal secretary. He hoped and prayed he was doing the right thing. There wasn't a great deal of crime on the island, so he wasn't sure who his clients would be, but as this was the only legal practice, he was looking forward to making a name for himself.

Troy was the happiest he'd been in years; he firmly believed he had become at one with the island. Surfing before and after work, getting to know the locals and spending quality time with Lucy was pretty much all he needed these days.

Troy was grateful that Lucielle Peyton-Smith, or Lucy as she preferred to be called, had cleaned his room at Clairemont Resort. He fell in love with her instantly and since then they had been inseparable— like teenagers in love.

After they'd been living together for a year, he decided to take the plunge and ask Lucy to marry him. Setting the scene, he booked a romantic dinner at the most luxurious restaurant on the island.

But as he sat there looking into the face he'd come to love, he was hit with second thoughts. He'd come such a long way over the last year, and Lucy was an integral part of his transformation, in fact he knew he wouldn't be here now without her calm and reassuring influence.

The tragic death of musician Lenni Maxwell the year before had taken its toll on Lucy. The media had been ruthless in their portrayal of Lenni's sordid life. Lucy was one of many who had had a torrid affair with Lenni, therefore it went without saying that the media had been merciless with everything they could drag up about their relationship, regardless of its truth.

Lucy's bountiful smile but vacant expression brought Troy back into the room, feeling somewhat embarrassed that he had zoned out of her conversation. He took a moment to immerse himself in the happy chatter of his surrounds.

"Sorry love, I didn't hear that; what were you saying?"

"I said: would you like to go for a walk on the beach?"

"Yes, I'd love that." Troy was thrilled with the suggestion of a leisurely stroll along the moonlit beach. That was a much more fitting place for his proposal; he wished he'd thought of it first.

Arm in arm they strolled the short distance to the beach. Taking off their shoes, they took a moment to lose themselves in the sensation of sand oozing through their toes, then the refreshing feel of the cool water as it lapped at their feet. They walked awhile before sitting on the sand, enjoying the breathtaking view along Clairemont beach.

As they sat side by side with only a breath of wind between them, Troy decided to pop the question.

"Lucy, we've been living together for the last year. I couldn't be happier, but I reckon it's time to take the next step and make our relationship more permanent. I'd be honoured if you'd consider being my wife. What do you think, will you marry me?" At the same time he reached into his pocket and pulled out a Tiffany box. He popped it open to reveal an impressive 2.00 carat heart-shaped diamond. Lucy gasped as she took in its beauty, but even in the moonlight he could tell the blood had drained from her face as she digested the proposal.

Instinctively she took the ring out of its box, and placed it on her finger, looking at it from every angle as it caught the rays of moonlight. She reluctantly put it back in the box, looked at Troy and, with a tear in her eye, she apprehensively replied: "This is so sudden; you've taken me by surprise. Is it OK if I think about it? As much as I love what we have, I didn't think we were getting that serious. I'm not saying no, but there's a lot to think about. You have become settled on the island, opening up your legal practice, and that's great, don't get me wrong, but I've spent my whole life trying to escape the island, and there is so much you don't know about me, I just need to reassess where I'm heading. Is that OK?"

"Lucy, I've been around, I've done things that would make your hair curl, so I can't imagine there is anything in your past that will stop me from loving you the way I do now. But yes, I want you fully committed to this relationship, so take as long as you need to think about what you want and where I fit in with your future."

They sat side by side in silence as the crash of the waves engulfed them in memories: troubled and deeply confronting memories.

Lucy was aware of Troy's past, she had witnessed first-hand how his past had collided with his present, and thankfully he came out OK. Yes, he lost the respect of his parents, but deep down he knew that separation had to happen for him to become his own person.

But Lucy's troubled past was one she wanted to forget, and every day she spent on the island she faced the possibility of walking into it head on.

The confines and security of the resort offered her the safety she needed to get through each day, but as she walked out into the depths of the island she could never predict what faced her.

This last year had seen a transformational change in her; she had been faithful to Troy, declining, for the first time ever, the advances of guests at the resort. She had always dreamed that being happily married would answer all her prayers, but now, in reality, would Troy leave her if he knew the truth about her past?

Troy broke the silence, "It's getting cold, let's head home, if you want to?"

"Of course I do," she responded, giving him a long lingering kiss.

He knew that kiss well; it was the *I want you* kiss. The hunger in his loins always stirred when she kissed him like that. Reassured that the outcome might be favourable, they walked back to the holiday home he rented, the one Lucy had helped him choose and decorate. The house that shared a year's worth of their happiest memories, the house she had grown to love.

Troy's attention to detail was one of his greatest assets. Today he wanted Lucy to know how much she meant to him. He'd spared no expense in creating the perfect illusion: the engagement ring spoke volumes, the dinner was carefully planned, and the bedroom had to reflect how he felt as well. To set the scene he'd called upon his good friend Ramon, the resort photographer, to help him make over the bedroom into a romantic work of art. The result was breathtaking.

Overstuffed feather pillows framed the king sized bed, but the wow factor was the huge red heart monogrammed in the centre of the lavishly crisp, white sheets that draped the oversized bed.

Beside the bed lay a chilled ice bucket, champagne and glasses, accompanied by a tray of strawberries and caviar.

The final touch was the path of red rose petals leading to and haphazardly scattered over the bed.

Troy had been almost certain that Lucy would jump at his proposal, so of course he wanted to finish the night off with a celebration the two of them would remember forever. Troy had forgotten about the champagne until Lucy entered the bedroom. It was her gasp that jolted him back to reality.

"Oh, Lucy, I'm sorry, I wanted the night to be perfect, let me get rid of it."

"No way—let's toast to the future, whatever that may be. Let's toast to your new legal practice. Let's toast to . . . possibilities," Lucy commanded as she handed Troy a glass of champagne.

They drank in silence, then lay cuddled in each other's arms. It was Lucy who made the first move—the long lingering kiss instigated a familiar routine that never failed to excite him. Expertly he moved around her body, addressing all of her needs. His kisses touched every part of her body, as she moved to the gentle rhythm. His fingers gently caressed her until she could hardly contain herself. Her body shuddered involuntarily after her fourth orgasm; Troy continued to show her just how much he loved her.

As she lay spent beside him, she thought long and hard about what to do.

Would she, could she tell Troy? How much could he take? She didn't know, and that was what scared her the most.

She knew what she had to do next, though. There was no escaping it now.

The following night she lied to Troy, telling him she needed to visit a friend. Lucy parked outside her arch-enemy's house;

she sat in the car for ages, too scared to walk up to the door, but knowing she had to. If she was going to make a commitment to Troy then she had to resolve this part of her life, and she had to do it now—she had to confront her worst enemy. She eventually plucked up the courage to knock on his door.

She hadn't expected him to answer the door so promptly. As they stood on the doorstep he abruptly asked, "What do you want?"

"I need to ask you some questions and I want honest answers, do you hear me, honest answers." Lucy tried to keep her composure.

"I've always been honest with you, Lucy."

"Now, you see, I know that's not the truth. I know what happened; I remember every vivid detail like it's etched in my brain. So I'm asking you for the last time, tell the truth," Lucy demanded.

"The truth about what, Lucy?"

"The truth about what you did all those years ago."

"I didn't do anything."

"Yes, you did, admit it, why can't you just admit it. I remember everything."

"I reckon your imagination is playing games with you, I didn't do a thing." He spat the words with vengeance.

"I won't take this any further if you only admit what you did, but if you continue to lie, then I may be forced to take this to the authorities, then you'll get what you deserve," Lucy threatened.

"Do what you like, Lucy, but are you sure you really want to go down that path? If you think you remember what I supposedly did, then why would you want to open that can of worms? This is a small island and I know where you live, you never know when our paths may cross. You needn't think that lawyer fella will be able to keep an eye on you

24/7."

"Stay away from me. Leave me the hell alone, don't follow me and don't ever come near my work or home," Lucy yelled at the now closed door.

Lucy was stunned, shocked even. How did he know about Troy? Had he been watching her, following her? Scared for her life, she ran to her car and frantically drove home. Once safely inside the confines of her home, she locked and bolted the front door, poured a glass of wine and disappeared into the bathroom to wash away the filth that was gnawing away at her skin.

She had no idea what to do next, her nightmare dreams had returned. She thought she was over it, but no, they continued to haunt her.

There was no way she could accept Troy's proposal. He would never marry her if he knew about her past. It was this island; she needed to get off it, more so now that *he* was obviously keeping an eye on her again. The thought of escaping the island was more frightening than actually going. She knew deep down that if she stepped foot on that ferry she would be signing her own death sentence.

Troy was her rock, her lover, her best friend, and her saviour. This last year had been the happiest she'd ever experienced, and she really wanted to continue just as they were. She was too ashamed to tell him anything about her past; she was too scared to lose him, to lose this, her sanctuary.

As usual, she climbed out of the cold bath no further ahead with her future plans. She had no one to talk to and no idea what to do next, but she knew she had to get rid of the demons of her past, that was a given.

CHAPTER THREE

The Innocence of Youth

For more than six months Hayley and Emily would spend Friday night sitting at the Clairemont Island pier, two fifteen-year-old high school students. Hayley had a very welcoming DD cup that was getting loads of attention, especially amongst the local boys. None of them interested Hayley; she was attracted to the older age group, the working boys, and the ones with money to spend. High school boys treated her like trash, they just wanted to have sex, and she couldn't be bothered with that. She was looking for a real man to take an interest in her, one that could afford to take her out, buy her things and treat her like a lady. Yeah, that's who she was looking for. She was after a man coming home from Sydney on a Friday night, after working on the mainland all week.

Hayley and Emily sat at the entrance to the pier, scanning everyone as they got off the ferry. After four weeks Hayley had spotted a worthy punter. She'd been watching him for a while now, she'd done her homework and now she was ready to make her first approach. Emily was fascinated with the planning and preparation Hayley had put into it. Hayley knew exactly what she wanted: someone with money.

The guy in question made his way off the ferry. Hayley quickly fell into step with him; by now she knew his name was Josh, he was twenty-two and an electrician. Best of all, he was single and not in a relationship with anyone on the island. She hoped there was nobody in Sydney, as that would ruin everything. As confidently as she could, she struck up a conversation with him.

"Josh, hi, my name is Hayley and I was told you are a math genius, I'm willing to pay anything if you could spare a couple of hours each weekend tutoring me. Please, I'll pay anything." She had chosen her outfit very carefully, covered up just enough to leave a little mystery. She was a very pretty girl, with a great body and big boobs that seemed to jump out of her outfit.

Josh stopped to look her over; she was very pleasing to the eye, and wow, what a set of knockers. He loved living in Sydney, but longed for the serenity of the island every weekend. He lived in the bungalow at the back of his parent's home, just behind the medical centre. His parents were away, a month cruising the Greek Islands. He couldn't understand why they would pay so much money to go half way around the world. In his opinion Clairemont Island was way better.

He didn't have anything else to do this weekend, he was seeing less and less of the locals he'd grown up with, as most of them had moved away or were in relationships. What harm could it do to tutor her a few hours each weekend? He loved math, and he'd make some money at the same time, hell, why not?

"Yeah, sure, when do you want to start?" Josh asked.

"How about right now, do you have any plans?" Hayley prayed that he didn't.

With a *what the hell* approach, he agreed to do it.

"Can we go to your place?" Hayley asked. "My parents are real tossers."

"OK, I suppose that'll be OK, do you have your books? What is it you're having trouble with exactly?"

"Yeah, books in here." She nodded to her bag and at the same time motioned to Emily to disappear.

Emily stopped dead in her tracks; she hadn't anticipated being dumped. What was she going to do now; she was supposed to be staying at Hayley's place all weekend.

"Bummer!" Emily muttered under her breath. She hadn't realised someone was right behind her. In fact he banged into her as she stopped so abruptly.

"What's the bummer, did you just get ditched?" a middle-aged gangly guy asked.

"Yeah, sort of, seems she got a better offer and I'm supposed to be staying at her place this weekend. I'm not sure what I'm supposed to do now."

"Tell you what, I'm heading over there to the pub for dinner, you are more than welcome to join me, I'll pay and you can order anything you want. My name is Oliver."

"I'm Emily . . . . . Yeah, why not?"

She had noticed a scar running down his face: she was too scared to mention it, but wondered what had happened to him. He smelt funny, was dressed in overalls and was kind of greasy looking, but he wasn't scary. She'd just have dinner and then go home.

They entered the pub, placed their order and chose a seat outside. It was eight-thirty p.m. He asked if she'd like a beer, but she declined, saying she wasn't old enough to drink. He was intrigued—she looked at least eighteen, but, hell, the kids these days, who can tell with the amount of makeup they wear, and he'd yet to see a teenager who didn't dress as if to say *take me I'm yours*.

Oliver drank a couple of beers as they ate their fish and

chips. The conversation was going really well, it had been a long time since someone had sat and talked with him. She was involved in a few groups and enjoyed school; she sounded like she was pretty good at her schoolwork, too.

After they finished eating, he asked if she would like to go for a walk; nowhere special, just walk and talk. She agreed and they walked a few times up and down the promenade, eventually making it to his house. He'd asked her on three different occasions if he could walk her home. Each time she refused, stating she didn't want to go home.

"Well, this is my home, I'm going in for a coffee, and you're more than welcome to join me if you want. You'll be perfectly safe, I promise. But you should know I play a wicked game of Crash Bandicoot."

"I've never played it, but I'm up to the challenge, if you are," Emily offered.

"OK, let's do it, come on in."

Oliver found the second remote, plugged it in and they started from level one. They'd only been playing about thirty minutes when his phone rang. He didn't say much, just the occasional yeah, then hung up.

He waited about five minutes before getting up and going into one of the bedrooms. The doorbell rang only the once, he walked over to the door, opened it, handed the person something, shut it, then sat back down to play again. Emily didn't give it much thought; she was too preoccupied in figuring out how the game worked.

More calls—same process. This happened about five times over a couple of hours. By now Emily was getting curious. Oliver down-played it, stating it was nothing.

"I'm heading outside for a smoke, back in a minute. You can keep playing if you want, I won't be long." Oliver said. He didn't offer her a cigarette; he wasn't having anything legal and he wasn't about to offer her what he was smoking, he wasn't that stupid.

"OK, do you have a Pepsi or something?" she asked.

"In the fridge, help yourself," Oliver said as he went outside.

He watched her through the window; she was quite attractive, her figure was starting to develop nicely. Dressed for her age she wasn't slutty looking. She was actually a nice wholesome-looking girl. The kind of girl you'd be proud to have as your daughter.

He finished his joint and made his way back into the lounge. She was still playing, but he noticed she was getting tired; after all it had just gone 1:00 a.m. He didn't have work the next day; he had the whole weekend off so he was in no rush to go to bed. He went to challenge her to another level, but he could tell she'd had enough; he grabbed a blanket and suggested she curl up on the sofa and get some sleep. He showed her where the bathroom was. Then told her he'd see her in the morning.

He awoke at 9:30 a.m. with his phone ringing. He answered it, went to the spare room where he stored his stash and, as he walked into the lounge, was surprised to see she was still there, curled up asleep on the sofa. He'd half expected her to have gone home.

He brewed a pot of coffee and waited for his first client of the day. The doorbell woke Emily. Startled, it took her a few minutes to register where she was.

"Morning, sleepyhead," Oliver said as he handed her a cup of coffee. "It's early, you can go back to sleep if you want. What time do you have to go home?" He wasn't being nosey; he just wanted to plan his day.

"Mum has gone to Sydney for a wedding and I'm supposed to be staying at Hayley's this weekend."

"No problem, you can stay here the weekend if you want, I promise you'll be safe. It'll be nice to have some company for

24

a change. What do you say?"

In a weird way he really wanted her to stay; he hadn't realised how much he enjoyed her company.

"If you think it's OK, I suppose I can. I do have a change of clothes in my bag, so if you don't mind I'd love to." Emily felt perfectly safe; he'd been a perfect gentleman. Emily wondered if this was the type of man Hayley was searching for. Oliver had certainly been her saviour last night.

"I think you should ring Hayley though, just to let her know that you are safe. The last thing you want is her ringing your mum."

"Yeah, good idea. I'll call her after I have a shower, is that OK?" Emily asked.

"Come, I'll show you where the towels are, if you need anything else give me a yell and I'll get it for you. I'm going to make breakfast, what would you like bacon, eggs, toast or cereal?"

"Just jam on toast, but I'd kill for another cup of coffee," she said as she closed the bathroom door.

Oliver was halfway through his breakfast when she sat down at the table, with toast, jam and coffee all waiting for her.

Emily called Hayley while Oliver was in the bathroom.

She had thought long and hard about what she would say about Oliver, deciding in the end not to mention him at all. She asked how it had gone with Josh, after which Hayley hogged the conversation for the next ten minutes. She assured Hayley she was safe and sound, home alone. Hayley was pleased because Josh had asked her to spend the weekend with him.

Emily was just finishing the dishes as Oliver walked back into the lounge. He looked quite different in the daylight; he'd tied his long hair back off his face, the scar now quite prominent, although not threatening. She asked how he'd got it.

"I kind of pissed off a few too many people when I was young and stupid, and this was their way of reminding me of what I owed them.

"Anyway, enough about me. Crank up that game and let's do it some damage, ah?"

"Sure thing. I think you're winning, even though you had so many interruptions last night. What was that all about?"

"Nothing for you to worry your pretty little head over. Let's start playing."

The day was lost in Crash Bandicoot. Oliver continued to get phone calls and mysterious visitors. They ordered pizza for lunch and Chinese for dinner. They drank an ocean of coffee and Pepsi. It was after dinner when Oliver realised he hadn't smoked a joint all day. Having someone to talk to had been the distraction he needed.

By ten in the evening, he was seeing double. Stating he couldn't play any longer, he was heading for bed. He tossed and turned, eventually admitting defeat. He had smoked a joint before going to bed every night for as long as he could remember. The drug calmed him enough to sleep peacefully all night. He got out of bed, trying not to wake Emily who was sleeping soundly on the sofa. He closed the back door, sat down in his chair behind his house, lit his joint and waited for the calmness to hit.

He wasn't aware she had followed him. Standing watching, she asked what he was smoking; it was different to anything she'd smelt before.

"Emily, sorry to wake you. Go back into the house, that's a good girl, I'll be in soon."

"Is that marijuana you're smoking? I've heard people talk about it; it's a drug isn't it?"

"Yeah, I suppose some people would call it a drug, but not me. It helps me sleep that's all. Now off you go, back to bed."

"No, I can't sleep. Maybe I should have one of those, will it help me sleep?"

"No, Emily, it won't help you sleep, now go inside."

"I want what you're having, please let me try it," Emily pleaded with him.

"I don't want to do this, Emily. You are too young to be taking this shit; it'll ruin your life." Oliver spoke from experience.

"I'm not too young, some of the boys at school are doing drugs, I've heard them talking about it. I really want to try it . . . please!" As she said the *please* she walked over to him and grabbed the joint out of his hand: inhaling fully, she choked on the smoke.

"See, I told you that you were too young. Enough. Now please go inside."

Emily refused to budge.

"No! Show me what to do, how do I smoke it?"

Oliver could tell there was no changing her mind.

He lit a new joint and showed her how to inhale and how to allow the smoke to do its work on the brain. To help her get in the zone, he placed a blanket on the ground and lay beside her as they shared the joint. They lay in silence for ages, just staring up at the stars, not talking, but lost in their own thoughts.

He carried her inside, laid her on the sofa, and covered her with the blanket. As he glanced down at her sleeping peacefully, he didn't expect to hear a peep out of her all night; she was well and truly wasted.

Sunday was an interesting day; it started with Emily running into his room early in the morning. She said she'd heard someone at the door. After checking inside and out he assured her there was nobody there. He was always careful, knowing the valuable commodity he carried in the house. He'd been robbed once before, but ever since Lenni

Maxwell's death—and the extra security he'd put in place— his clients appreciated he was the only supplier in town and, if he got busted, they would all suffer. On Clairemont Island he held the monopoly, his client base was growing steadily and he was sitting very pretty. He wasn't playing the big time, he'd learned to stay small, stay safe, and stay under the radar.

Emily settled back into a deep sleep. She didn't wake till after ten in the morning. Starving, she reckoned she could eat a horse, but settled for a few pieces of toast instead.

Oliver, knowing he had to meet a new client—and he never did that in his own home—was wondering what to do with her while he was away. He asked if there was something she was comfortable in cooking for dinner as she didn't seem to be in a hurry to go home. She checked his fridge, freezer and pantry, surveyed the ingredients and told him she would make lasagna. Great choice. He left her to it, saying he'd be gone about an hour.

Her lasagna was a bit runny, she'd forgotten to thicken the sauce, but hey, anyone could make that mistake, it still tasted pretty good.

By eight in the evening, he had to force her to leave. He literally had to push her out the door. She did so only after he promised she could come back again the following weekend.

True to her word, the following Friday night she was waiting for him at his front door. Only this time she didn't challenge him to any PlayStation games, well not right away. Instead she wanted to talk. To talk about drugs.

She hadn't mentioned the weekend to anybody, opting instead to keep it a secret.

What consumed her week were the conversations she'd overheard, conversations she'd normally not listen to. She wasn't entirely stupid: she'd figured out that Oliver was dealing drugs.

By midweek, she was confused. Some of her classmates were boasting about smoking weed; they described how they felt and what they did. It was nothing like what Emily had experienced, so she wasn't sure if they were lying or not. She almost ran over to Oliver's home right away to ask him, but changed her mind and decided to wait till Friday night.

"Emily, it's like this, people experience drugs differently, although most people feel relaxed, euphoric or at peace, some have the opposite effect where they get angry or agitated. Are they lying? Possibly not. Do you know who they got it from?

"No, I didn't ask, do you think I should? I mean, they don't even know I was listening; hell they don't even know I exist."

"Look, I know the quality of my stock is first class, and that makes a big difference in the reaction people have. The better the quality, the better the experience. If they can't afford good quality stock they're asking for trouble, please tell them that, OK! There is shit out there that will kill them, especially if they don't know what they're looking for." Oliver looked her square in the eye, pleading for her to pass this valuable information on to them.

"OK, I will," Emily reassured him.

The weekend together was more subdued this time around. Oliver begrudgingly allowed her to smoke some more. She was getting the hang of it and she looked so serene when she was high.

The following week at school she waited for an opportunity to enter the conversation. She didn't have to wait long. Monday sports period out on the oval playing footy she added her two cents. Taken aback by her comment, they demanded she show up with the goods; if her stash was a higher quality, they wanted to try it.

Monday night she made her way to Oliver's house, hoping he'd have a solution for her, cos she was still in shock, wondering what the hell she'd done. Now she'd spoken, they expected her to turn up with the goods.

Oliver sent her armed with a couple of joints, with the proviso to be extremely cautious about what she said and where they smoked it. She was never to reveal where she got it. She was never to mention his name or identify that she knew him.

True to her word, Emily kept his identity a secret. She left his house every Sunday night with a small tin of joints. Oliver had asked her to be extremely careful and to pay attention to who asked her for them and who enjoyed them the most, as they would be the ones she would work with when the time was right, whatever that meant, Emily didn't care, she just did what Oliver told her. She cared a great deal for him and didn't want to spoil their friendship.

He was too important to her now. She'd never met anyone like him. He listened to her, conversed with her about anything and she could tell he genuinely cared for her. In a weird way, Emily thought she could be falling in love with him; he was so different to the boys at her school. She now knew why Hayley did all that preparation and planning to get Josh. But Oliver was way older than Josh. In fact, he was probably as old as her parents, but somehow that didn't seem to bother her, she didn't see their relationship as weird. Her parents, on the other hand, seemed foreign; they would never talk to her like Oliver did, and conversations on topics like drugs and sex would never be mentioned in their house—no way, never.

In truth, her parents didn't speak to each other since their separation and neither was interested in speaking to her. They were both lost in their own world, facing their own demons. Emily could have been on a different planet and they wouldn't have noticed.

CHAPTER FOUR

Hidden Meaning

Ex-Police Officer Gabby Saintclaire, now manager of Clairemont Resort, grabbed her usual table at her favourite café along Clairemont Promenade. Early morning was the best time to sit outside—sheltered from the coastal sea breeze, the shade sail protected them from the harsh sun. Tuesday morning coffee had become a regular pastime for Gabby ever since Katrina had moved to the island. Detective Inspector Katrina Reid moved there after the murder of famous musician Lenni Maxwell the previous year. Until then, there hadn't been any crime to speak of and, with Sydney only four hours by ferry, there hadn't been a need to have a police presence on the island.

Fortunately, Gabby, with the help of her husband, Michael, the resort security officer, James, and Dr. Terrence Scott (Scotty), had managed to solve the crime before a cyclone hit, and they kept the murderer in custody until Katrina arrived from Sydney three days later.

But the powers that be deemed it necessary to provide a

higher level of security to the island and, seeing as Katrina had wrapped everything up quickly after Lenni's murder, they asked if she would like the post. It didn't seem to matter how many times she explained that Gabby had had everything under control before she'd arrived.

Over-qualified for the role, she wondered if it had something to do with the affair she was having at the time with a married senior member of parliament. As a way of escaping the scandal, she took up the offer to get away from the cesspit of scum in Sydney, and welcomed the idea of a sea change.

Gabby and Katrina became close friends, in addition to having the police force in common. They were almost the same age, shared similar interests and had the same weird sense of humour. The main difference was Katrina's devastating track record with men. She attracted some very interesting characters, and this always made the conversation on their coffee dates the more enjoyable.

Thanks to the many years in the police force, Gabby had learned to read people really well. It was a skill that, once learned, you never forgot and, at times like this, she was thankful for. As she observed Katrina making her way to the café, Gabby could tell that she was troubled.

"Is something wrong?" Gabby asked.

"Actually, yes. I've noticed signs of drugs around and wonder how they're getting onto the island. Apart from private yachts, the ferry is the only way on and off this island, unless it's being manufactured here. Have you seen or heard anything?" Katrina posed the question.

"No, not a thing. I must be blind. I haven't noticed anything. After Lenni died it came out that his parties offered every drug imaginable. It was never revealed how the drugs appeared. Was that investigated at the time of the court case?"

"No, and to be perfectly honest, it was never questioned. I mean, you guys caught the murderer, Grant Woodham, and although Lenni had drugs in his system there was never any substance found at his house. I think I need to do some surveillance," Katrina said.

"That's a great idea, where will you start?" Gabby knew she shouldn't have asked, but the ex-cop in her couldn't be silenced.

"Just between you and me—I mean it, this is strictly confidential—I'm going to be keeping a very close eye on all the ferry crew. I'll start with the locals first, see what I can uncover, and then I'll talk to the guys on the mainland and see if they can assist with surveillance of the Sydney crew. I may have to bring over one of the dogs for a while, just to do some sniffing around.

"To begin with, I'd like to drive all over the island. I know some areas are secluded, but I want to see for myself what looks legit or suss. Would you like to join me?"

"Seriously? Hell, yeah! Just tell me when." Gabby knew the cop in her was always on duty, regardless of what she told people. After six years, it was still as strong as the day she left the force.

"How about this afternoon? I'll pick you up at 2:00 p.m." Katrina was pleased to have Gabby to share the drive and a second person to brainstorm with.

"It's a done deal, see you then." The two stood to leave the café; air kissed and went their separate ways. Gabby back to Clairemont Resort and Katrina to the small but inviting building that now housed the police station.

Gabby couldn't believe her luck. She didn't miss being a police officer, but she certainly missed the work; she loved the rewarding feeling associated with solving problems, and there were many cases she had laid claim to solving over her twelve years in the force.

Michael knew something was up with Gabby as soon as he saw her waltz into the resort.

"You look like a mischievous toddler, what have you been up to?" Michael asked his wife. He hadn't seen her with a smile like this for ages. He was curious to find out what had transpired over coffee with Katrina.

"Come into the office and I'll tell you all about it." Gabby grabbed her husband's arm and pulled him into the office they shared.

"Just between you and me, Katrina asked me to do some surveillance with her. She wants me to show her parts of the island she hasn't been to and she's going to start surveillance on the ferry crew. Seems she's trying to figure out how drugs are getting onto the island, and she wants my help. We're going out this afternoon. You won't miss me for a few hours will you?" She was so excited she totally forgot she already had a job.

"Yes, that'll be fine, but just remember you are no longer a police officer, we run a resort now. It's Katrina's job to maintain safety and security on the island, not yours, OK?"

"Yeah, I know, but I can be another pair of eyes for her, show her parts of the island she's unaware of. That's all. I promise," with that Gabby retired to their apartment in the resort to get ready.

Michael knew he was wasting his time—she was on a mission and until Katrina had found the source of the drug supply there would be no stopping Gabby. She was in her element; that's what he loved about her.

2:00 p.m. didn't come soon enough; she had called Katrina and suggested she pick her up in the resort car instead of using the police car—less conspicuous.

Katrina was waiting for Gabby outside the police station. Gabby was pleased to see Katrina wearing civilian clothes. They spent ages investigating the remote parts of the island, but unfortunately couldn't see anything out of the ordinary; it didn't look as if there were any tyre tracks or signs of access to dense forest areas.

The ferry was due, so they stopped at the entrance of the pier to observe the crew. They watched the passengers disembark and waited another fifteen minutes until the ferry crew made their way down the pier. As each one passed, Gabby revealed what she knew about them, which wasn't much.

"So, who are we going to follow first?" Gabby asked.

"That guy there, he looks pretty shady."

Gabby didn't know his name; in fact, she'd never seen him before. He was ferry crew, because he'd exited the ferry with the crew and he was filthy dirty. They watched the short, stocky, red haired young guy make his way to a parked car, a beat up, rusted red Cortina. Katrina was the first to notice the overlarge backpack.

"That bag looks pretty full: apart from his lunch, he's wearing his jacket so what could he possibly have inside to bulk it up so much?" Katrina asked.

"Not sure. Do you want to pull him over and find out?" The cop in Gabby was on duty.

"No, let's just follow and see where he goes."

They waited until he was out of the car park and he'd driven past them before they turned the car around and slowly started to follow.

He weaved around the island until finally parking outside a small bungalow. The For Sale sign out the front was a godsend. They decided to drop in to see real estate owner Susan Olsen and find out who owned the house.

As they walked up to the real estate office, Susan was hanging pictures of new properties in the window.

"Hiya, Susan how's business?" Gabby asked.

"Pretty good, it's always busy this time of the year, seems

everyone wants to sell up and get away from the island before the influx of summer tourists."

"Actually, would you like a cuppa? I was just going to make one," Susan asked.

"Love to, lead the way." Gabby said.

"What do you know about the bungalow on Stevenson Street?" Katrina asked while Susan made the coffee.

"Just listed that this week. The owners want to sell as they have made an offer on a property in Brisbane. Are you interested?"

"Maybe. Do the owners live in it, or is it a rental?" Katrina asked.

"It's a rental. If you want it as an investment, I can tell you that the current tenant is happy to stay on, he's really good. He looks after the place and always pays on time. He's one of my best tenants."

"Is there any chance we can have a look through? I'm thinking of buying on the island and I love the look of it from the outside," Katrina asked.

"Let me make a call and arrange a time, he works the ferry, so not sure what shift he's on," Susan responded.

"Hello, Adam, it's Susan Olsen. I know it's short notice, but wondered if it's possible to bring someone through, when is a good time for you? OK, if you're sure, that would be lovely. I'll just ask them if they want to come now." Gabby and Katrina nodded in agreement and Susan told Adam to expect them in ten minutes.

"How's that for luck?"

Susan drove them to the bungalow and, true to her word, the small two-bedroom bungalow was immaculately presented. Adam welcomed them in and then retired outside to the courtyard to read the paper and enjoy a beer.

Gabby and Katrina scrutinised the house from top to bottom and couldn't see anything that would cast suspicion of him as a drug dealer. They took the opportunity to speak to him as they stepped outside to see the modest courtyard.

"Adam, do you mind if I ask about your neighbours, are they nosey or do they leave you alone? The reason I ask is that where I am at the moment my elderly neighbours are real busybodies and know everything I do. It drives me insane, which is why I'm looking to move. I really don't want to buy a place and be stuck with the same kind of nosey neighbours." Katrina was digging for information, not that Adam was aware of what she was doing

"Na, they're a really nice family. Sometimes I'll stay in Sydney on the weekends and Trish next door will come and feed my cat, like she did last night, as I stayed overnight; she has a key to the house. She's not nosey, just a really nice neighbour that you can count on if you're stuck. She works from home, so keeps an eye on things. You wouldn't have any problems with them, and the house on the other side is hardly ever used as they live in Melbourne and only come over a few weeks every year."

"What's your plan, when this sells? Are you staying on the island, or does the mainland beckon you?" Gabby asked.

"Na, I'm staying here, I love the island. I'm sure Susan can find me somewhere else, but if it's sold as an investment, I'd be happy to stay on."

They thanked Adam for allowing them to look through the bungalow at short notice and went back to the office where Susan noticed her daughter Emily making her way in the opposite direction from their home. "Where on earth is she going? She promised me she was studying with friends after school. Her friends don't live in that direction. Looks like we'll be having words again tonight."

"Well, Katrina, what do you think? It's a lovely bungalow and really well priced for the market."

"It certainly is. Can I think about it, after all this is the first one I've looked at? In fact, until I drove past it I hadn't even considered moving, but there was something about that place that captured my attention." Katrina was as truthful as she could be under the circumstances.

"Sure thing, let me know your decision, and I'm sure Adam wouldn't mind if you wanted to go back and have another look."

As Gabby and Katrina drove back to the police station, they noticed Emily again. Dressed in school uniform with backpack strapped over her shoulder, she was making her way to the outskirts of town. Wondering where she could possibly be going, there were only a handful of houses out there, Gabby decided to follow her. Emily finally stopped and went inside a modest weatherboard.

A middle-aged gentleman entered the house a few minutes later.

"Do you know who he is?" Katrina asked.

"Yes, I do. I must say I'm not sure why Emily would have anything to do with him. His name is Oliver Smith, he's lived on the island for years and he also works the ferry.

"To my knowledge he lives alone, but I may be mistaken. Can we sit here awhile; I want to see how long she stays?" Gabby had an uneasy feeling in the pit of her stomach.

They waited patiently out of sight for three hours until finally Emily emerged dressed in jeans and tee shirt. Alarm bells were ringing loudly. Both Katrina and Gabby noticed her change of clothing and were wondering why she would change out of her school uniform and into civilian clothes while in his home.

"Any thoughts?" Katrina asked.

"I'm not sure. I know things aren't that good at home since Susan and Dwayne separated, but I'm at a loss to understand why she would be going to see Oliver and why the need to change clothes?"

"Do you think there's something sexual happening?" Katrina asked.

"I hope not, but hey, it's entirely possible. Weirder things have happened."

"I need to get back to the resort, Michael will be wondering what's happened to me. How about we sit on everything we've seen today. Let's talk tomorrow." Gabby felt as though the wind had been knocked out of her.

She loved detective work, but had forgotten the emotional churning it caused.

CHAPTER FIVE

Clairemont Ferry

Public Relations Manager for *This Could Be Your Life* magazine, Terry Henderson, had been having a long-time fling with model Molly Williams, but because of their contractual obligations with the magazine, they had kept their relationship a secret.

When Terry was asked to project manage the photo shoot on Clairemont Island, he jumped at the chance, especially when he heard that Molly was to be one of the models for the shoot.

On-board a flight from Los Angeles to Sydney, seated side-by-side in business class; the long exhausting journey didn't seem to faze them too much. They sipped their drinks, ate restaurant quality food, and enjoyed the luxury of massage as their seats ground away the tension of the day. They watched inflight movies, then changed into complimentary pyjamas as the cabin crew reclined their seat flat into a bed, and covered them in a crisp sheet and blanket as they settled into slumber.

Terry had worked for the magazine for fifteen years; as a

well-respected member of the team he was allowed certain perks, although flying business class was not one of them. Company policy stated all crew was to fly together and be allocated the same-standard shared-room accommodation. But when Terry learned of the travel time, he opted to pay the difference for business class, and so did Molly. They also opted to keep that to themselves. They actually believed they would get away with it, last on and first off at the other end, nobody would know—or so they thought.

Cameron Collins, photographer for the magazine, sat perched upright in his seat, the one he'd become very familiar with over the fifteen and a half-hour flight from LA. Cramped, uncomfortable seats and disgusting pre-heated inflight catering had left him with a disgusted taste in his mouth.

Anger was brewing; he could feel it churning in the pit of his stomach. Clutching a cup of tasteless coffee, he was waiting for the descent into Sydney, when the curtains would open and he could positively confirm his suspicion—not that he needed to, he already knew the answer. Many times during the flight, he had walked back and forth up the aisles and in doing so he'd identified that Molly Williams and Terry Henderson were not seated with the rest of the magazine crew in economy. In truth, he'd probably have accepted it, had it just been Terry up in business class, but he couldn't come to terms with Molly sitting up there. What gave her the right? She was only a model and had only worked for the magazine for a few years.

Having been fed, hair and makeup artist Katy Pringle couldn't stop annoying Cameron; she was excited about flying into a country she had only read about. Neither of them could believe their luck. This photo shoot was the trip of a lifetime, the magazine had thought long and hard about whom to send. Katy was especially grateful to be chosen;

after all they could have hired a local makeup artist. She was feeling pretty damn pleased with herself—here she was on-board her first international flight.

The captain broke into their conversation with his early morning announcement.

"Good morning, I'm Captain Greig and on behalf of myself and the Qantas crew we would like to welcome you to Australia. Local time in Sydney is 6:20 a.m. It's currently eighteen degrees with just a slight breeze, there's a ten percent chance of a thunderstorm later this afternoon with a predicted top of twenty-two degrees. Now please settle yourselves in for landing; we have clearance to make our descent and should have you ready to depart the aircraft by 7:00 a.m."

Excellent, not long now, thought Cameron as Katy climbed over him in an effort to make a last-minute dash to the toilet.

Focusing on the closed curtain, waiting for it to open, Cameron's thoughts drifted to his fiancée Anthea. They'd lived together for a few years and he thought their relationship was pretty good, that was until three days ago. Cameron was stopped at the lights, waiting for them to turn green, just a block from their modest but comfortable apartment in Pasadena. While patiently waiting for the lights to change, he glanced in the direction of a popular restaurant; standing outside on the sidewalk, in full view, he saw his fiancée in the embrace of another man. He'd watched this middle-aged well-dressed man walk up to Anthea and they embraced and kissed: this was not just an introductory embrace. What Cameron witnessed was a full-on pash that lingered for too long to be coincidental. They obviously knew each other, but how? Cameron certainly didn't know him; he'd never seen him before. It was definitely Anthea; she was dressed in the same outfit she left the house in that morning. The lights changed and he was jolted back by the honk of a horn nudging him to move it.

With a last glance toward the restaurant, he noticed they were still entwined in each other's arms, only now moving inside the restaurant. He knew he would have to say something before heading to Australia, if he didn't, it would eat him up.

When she came home that night, complaining about being overworked and underpaid, he asked about her day; she said it was just another boring day at the office. He asked if she made it out for lunch, but she reassured him she hadn't. In fact, she had to ask one of her colleagues to grab her a sandwich because she had deadlines that she was failing to meet. She quickly added it was just as well he was going away as it would give her the chance to do all this extra work. So she lied to him: he wondered what else she'd been lying about.

The A380 landed and taxied to the terminal, but it was when the unbuckle seat sign dinged that Molly and Terry, who were seated side by side, rose to grab their bags from the overhead compartment. Bingo! Cameron thought as a wicked smile invaded his face.

Getting through customs was actually quite quick compared to the process at LAX, which was good because Cameron was chomping at the bit to catch up with Molly. It helped that Molly had inadvertently left her boarding pass in the pocket of her business class seat, which Cameron had noticed and grabbed for insurance. He didn't want to speak to her in front of anyone else; he had decided it was his fight, his argument, and his problem. He did want to get this first accusation out of the way here at the airport, before they jumped on the ferry to Clairemont Island.

Cameron had not slept on the flight; he had far too much on his mind. What was he going to do about Anthea? Was she having an affair on him, and what would he do now that he had physical proof that Molly and Terry had breached company policy?

Cameron did not get the opportunity to confront Molly at the airport or during their minivan taxi ride to the ferry terminal.

After they boarded the ferry, Cameron was so mesmerised with the city skyline that he totally lost himself in capturing what he could see of Sydney through the eyes of his camera. It wasn't until the ferry was well out to sea, making its way out to the South Pacific, that he went indoors. A slight chill from the ocean breeze had given him the second wind he needed to get through the rest of the day.

He quickly found the rest of the crew seated around a booth to the far side of the bar. As they squished further into the booth to make room for Cameron, he noticed Molly and Terry at the far end in deep conversation with Robbie and Brenton, the male models for the shoot. There was far too much chatter nearby to hear what they were talking about. With a beer and some nuts, he settled down to talk to the rest of the crew. He thought he could let it go, but the more he glanced in their direction the more agitated he became, eventually opting to go outside to cool off.

As he went to exit outside, he pushed the door so vigorously he knocked over one of the ferry staff, a middle-aged, longhaired, gangly guy.

"I'm sorry, are you OK?" Cameron asked apologetically as he attempted to pick the guy up off the deck.

"Yeah, good mate, but you're packing a hell of a punch, what did that door ever do to you?" Oliver Smith replied.

"Nothing, just a bit pissed that's all."

"No kidding, that's pretty obvious. Are you hoping the breeze will cool you down?"

"Maybe, but reckon I'm past that, I may need something a hell of a lot stronger." Cameron muttered, but loud enough that Oliver heard him.

"Are you thinking something a lot stronger than what you can find in the bar?" Oliver enquired.

Oliver had just celebrated his fiftieth birthday; it was a dismal reflection of his life. Nobody celebrated it with him. Nobody cared.

Drugs had been a part of his life since he was fifteen years old. He started dealing drugs when he was introduced to 'the family' at seventeen. The family he thought was going to keep him embosomed, in fact turned out to be the death of him—turning their back on him and leaving him for dead. He fled to Sydney to escape and begin a new life. This new life was to be drug free, but he was an idiot, he had no willpower. His overwhelming desire for sex and drugs couldn't be tamed. Just a few days after landing in Sydney he met a retired prostitute in the lift of his hotel; she lived in the room opposite him. Needless to say, a prostitute never retires. She came with an open door, a vacant bed, a drawer full of cocaine and time to kill. Back in the habit he was oblivious to the fact it ruled his life. His habit forced him to work and, like today, every crossing brought him someone who needed it just as much as he did.

"What are you suggesting? Cameron had his suspicion, but wondered if they were on the same page.

"I was just heading out for my break. If you'd like to join me, I reckon I can offer you something that may take the edge off that frustration of yours. Up to you, though."

"Hell, yeah. Lead the way." Cameron followed Oliver as he made his way around the back of the stacked deck chairs. Thankfully the chill of the wind had sent all other passengers inside.

Away from prying eyes, Oliver and Cameron spent over an hour enjoying a couple of joints as they talked about life on Clairemont Island. Oliver gave Cameron heaps of ideas on where to shoot for maximum scenery and mentioned his ability to supply any substance Cameron may want while on the island.

They talked about Anthea and the supposed affair. Oliver listened, then responded.

"The way I see it, if she is having an affair, then you'd be a fool to ignore the beauties you'll see on the island. If she isn't having an affair, why lie to you about working over lunch when she clearly wasn't, and why would she be pashing some other fella? Sounds pretty obvious to me, so why not enjoy yourself while you're here? Let your hair down and have a great time."

Oliver's advice on the Molly/Terry dilemma took him by surprise; Oliver took a different view of the situation.

"If it was me, I wouldn't worry too much about getting even with them. Life is too short to be bothered by something that could potentially ruin the photo shoot and your trip here. File it. Leave it for a rainy day, so to speak. See what else manifests—you never know when you could use this to your advantage, but not yet, it's too soon." Oliver retreated back to work.

Making his way to the cafeteria, Cameron was starving. He surveyed the menu. Checking his watch, he calculated there was still time to order the big breakfast before the ferry to Clairemont Island Pier arrived and docked.

Lingering over his cup of coffee, waiting patiently for his food to arrive, he scanned everyone seated in the cafeteria. He noticed an alarming number of females seated by themselves; Cameron realised this trip might provide him some fun after all. Mentally thanking Oliver for putting his mind to rest about Anthea, he graciously accepted his plate of food. As he ate, he observed the women around him, eventually settling on a voluptuous young blonde. She had striking features and healthy long blonde hair, that looked natural not bleach blonde, a beautiful smile, nice white teeth, and high cheekbones, but it was her eyes that intrigued him the most. She was reading a book, but occasionally she would glance up and it was then that he noticed their colour, a brilliant bright blue, the colour of the ocean. She was blessed with a great looking body as well. Hard to tell as she was sitting, but he guessed she would be close to 186 cm. tall. He could tell from the way she held herself in her seat that she had excellent posture, and oh, she didn't appear to be wearing a wedding ring.

With a fresh cup of coffee, he made his way to her table. Immersed in the book, she didn't immediately notice he had sat opposite her until he spoke.

"Sorry to bother you, I wondered if you've ever been to Clairemont Island before. This is my first visit and I was just reading up on what to do there. Then it occurred to me to ask other people what they intended to do on the island, hoping that will help me make decisions."

Taken aback by his approach, Faith Ash, a Clairemont Island resident took a moment to scrutinise him before offering her answer. He was a good-looking guy, probably around the same age as her, with short brown hair, brown eyes. A cute smile with a distinct five o'clock shadow—she wasn't sure if he was trying to grow it into something or if he simply hadn't shaved for a couple of days. The bags under his eyes indicated he may have travelled a distance, and she was right. Detecting an accent, she decided it would be quicker just to ask him where he came from, rather than try to pinpoint it herself.

"Is that an American accent I can hear?" Faith decided to take the conversation further.

"Canadian born, but I live in Los Angeles, thanks for asking. What about yourself, where do you hail from? Cameron asked.

"I'm born and bred on Clairemont Island," Faith said. "I live there with my twin sister. My parents moved to Australia a few years ago, but we love it so much we couldn't leave." My name is Faith, by the way."

"Faith, I'm Cameron, it's nice to meet you. Seems to me like you'd be the best person to tell me what to do and where to go on the island." He responded as he reached out to shake her hand.

"Sure thing, how long are you here for?"

"Eight days, but I've got a five-day photo shoot in the middle of it. So, realistically, not much time at all."

"Sounds interesting. My sister and I have done modeling before, one of our many jobs. Who is the photo shoot for? Are you a model?" Faith enquired.

"No, I'm not a model, I'm a photographer and this is a shoot for *This Could Be Your Life* magazine. Have you heard of them?"

"No, sorry. But if you need some extra models, give me a call; Fay and I can help out. If you want I can show you my portfolio."

"Yes, that would be excellent. How about later today, what do you have planned?" Cameron knew he would be busy making sure everything was ready to go for the shoot, but he was sure he could squeeze her in sometime later in the day.

"I don't have anything else on today; I can swing past your hotel anytime you want. We'll dock at the pier around 2:00 p.m. How about I let you rest up and call in after dinner, say eight?" Faith suggested.

"Better still, how about I take you out for dinner? You can pick me up at Clairemont Resort at 6:00 p.m. and take me somewhere nice, show me some of the sights. Here's my business card." As Cameron handed her his card, he was jolted by electricity. Pulling his hand backwards, he apologised.

"Sorry about that, it seems we have made a connection, so to speak."

"Actually I'd like to connect in other ways if you're up to it," Faith nervously suggested.

"I'm certainly up for anything; what are you thinking?

"Well, we still have some time till we dock, and I can almost guarantee that nobody will be outside till we get much closer to the island. If you don't mind getting a bit cold, I know where we can get better acquainted."

"You've convinced me, lead the way."

Cameron and Faith made their way outside, heading in the opposite direction from the one he had ventured with Oliver earlier in the crossing. Cameron gathered Faith had done this more than once, she knew exactly where she was going. He didn't care, he was going to enjoy this trip, no regrets, no fiancée, and nothing was going to get in his way of having the time of his life. Starting right now.

Secluded from sight behind some equipment, he took his time getting to know Faith Ash, every little bit of her. Oblivious to the temperature, she encouraged the removal of her dress. As he raised the flimsy material over her breasts, he paused for a moment to fondle each of them and allowed his tongue to tease her nipples. Using the wall of what sounded like the equipment room, he leaned Faith against it as he steadied himself with the rhythm of the ferry. His lips alternated between her breasts and her mouth and he was taken by surprise as her hand found its way under his clothes to locate its rock hard target. His hand crept its way down her body, removing her panties and finding its final destination. It wasn't long before their rhythm gained in intensity. She lowered his pants and, baring his butt to the elements, he quickly entered her and together they enjoyed the final leg of the journey as the ferry made its way toward Clairemont Island.

The ferry docked on time and the magazine crew boarded the Clairemont Resort minivan and was transported to the resort.

The registration process was seamless; each crewmember was directed by company policy to share rooms. Terry and Cameron were to share a room. Terry asked Cameron if he objected to having the room to himself. Terry did not desire to share a room and knew he would be spending all his time with Molly; thankfully she had been allocated a room to herself. He just wanted Cameron's reassurance that he'd keep it quiet—quiet from the crew and the company.

Cameron jumped at the chance to have a single room, after all he knew exactly how he was going to be using it, and that certainly didn't equate to a single body in his bed. He was going to bed anything that walked. He'd been living with his fiancée Anthea a few years now, and he'd been faithful. That was until today, but she started it, her infidelity started this whole thing. It really hurt: the more he thought of her the more he wanted to get even, so yeah, a single room was exactly what he wanted. It was also a second piece of ammunition he could use on Terry if he ever needed it.

"Oh, Terry, before you go, I just wanted to let you know I spoke to a beautiful young woman on the ferry. She lives here on the island and she and her twin sister are models. She's dropping off her portfolio to me tonight."

"Cameron, don't go promising her anything, OK? Let's discuss this before any decisions are made. You do understand the last thing we need is to piss the locals off. How about we meet down in the restaurant for breakfast, say eight am? We are scouting locations from 10:00 a.m., so we'll have plenty of time to talk about it then."

"OK, sounds like a plan; see you then. For now, I'm having a shower and going to get some sleep, the flight was a nightmare, those seats played havoc with my back. How about you, did you enjoy the flight?" Cameron knew he was only looking for some acknowledgment about the flight, but the response from Terry of 'same' was better than listening to his lies.

Cameron opened the door to his room. Moving through the galley kitchen into the tastefully decorated lounge, he walked directly to the balcony door and opened it to reveal an expansive lush green lawn and quaint English gardens. He looked back into the room and was suitably impressed. With beige lounge suites and pale blue tub chairs positioned perfectly around a glass table, the gas fireplace on the wall under the giant TV added an element of luxury he hadn't seen before in a hotel room.

To the right of the lounge, both bedrooms were decorated in the same soft tan and cream furnishings; king sized beds adorned with crisp white sheets; pale blue cushions and throw rugs complemented the ambience.

Cream and pale blue tiles sheathed the walls of the luxurious bathroom. The double shower took up the far wall, but the statement piece was the slipper claw foot freestanding bathtub. I'm certainly going to be relaxing in you, he thought, as he took in the opulence of the room.

Choosing the bedroom with the balcony, he opened the door to allow the gentle breeze to flow through. He climbed between the crisp white sheets, only to toss and turn. He felt relaxed, so why couldn't he sleep? So much was going around his head—after thirty minutes he admitted defeat, he dressed and went to explore the resort, eventually settling in to enjoy a nice cold beer in the Zanzabar, the resort hotel.

There was a steady stream of guests mingling in the bar; during the quiet times he struck up a conversation with Andrew, the bar manager.

"How long have you lived on the island?" Cameron asked Andrew.

"Gosh, that would be about seven years, seems forever. I was fortunate to have come here for a friend's wedding, and I fell in love with the energy of the island. I just knew I had to live here, and when I mentioned it to the bar manager he offered me a job. I went back to Manila where I was working at Raffles Hotel, gave them my notice and moved here. I can't imagine I will ever leave; you'd be surprised how many people come here and never leave.

Andrew got busy serving guests and Cameron started watching a Yankee Dodgers game. Unfortunately, it was a repeat, but that didn't stop him enjoying it again. Andrew remembered to inform Cameron when it was 6:00 p.m., time for him to meet Faith for his dinner date.

Cameron entered reception just as Faith walked into the resort, with her was her twin sister Fay. They had an air of elegance as they walked in unison. They looked stunning as their long blonde hair bounced with every step. He felt a twinge in his loins as he took in their beauty. Faith introduced her sister and they walked Cameron to their car. Cameron couldn't take his eyes off them; it took a while for him to find some sign to tell them apart. When they smiled, one had a wider smile than the other: he was to learn that Faith had whiter teeth, her lips were fuller and her smile was more radiant.

The restaurant they chose was on the other side of the island—a place the young folk liked to hang out, a place where you could openly partake in the pleasures of many sins. The food was pretty good too.

A short ten-minute drive around some breathtakingly beautiful scenery left Cameron gob-smacked. He'd never seen anything like it before; no wonder the magazine wanted them to come half way around the world for the photo shoot. He suddenly 'got it'—his eye for detail had his mind racing in every direction as he took in the scenery.

Grabbing a table outside, the three got acquainted. Faith, true to her word, had bought her portfolio; there was no need for Fay to bring hers, it was virtually a duplicate. He was about to hire them, when he remembered Terry's words. Instead, he told them he'd show Terry the following morning and get back to them with an answer.

"That's perfectly fine, I understand. Let's enjoy our meal, a few drinks and I'll drop you back to the resort whenever you want," Faith replied.

The next four hours were a blur. Cameron wasn't sure if it was his lack of sleep, the few too many beers or the cocaine they snorted after dinner, but as the girls delivered him back to the resort, he invited them in for a nightcap and was pleased they agreed.

He'd never had a threesome before; he was impressed at how they worked as a team, satisfying each other, twins sharing the experience individually and together as one. He'd never watched two girls make love to each other. He stopped them midstream, he couldn't contain himself any longer, it was beautiful to watch, but he wanted to be part of the journey, to make them come as they had made him, time and time again. The night was long and exciting; one he hoped and prayed would be repeated.

Around 3:00 a.m. Cameron woke as Faith and Fay dressed to go home. The sight of them set him off again, but they restrained him, promising to see him again later that day.

CHAPTER SIX

A Distant Memory

In a crumpled heap, lying lethargically on her bedroom floor, sixteen-year-old Emily Olsen was a blubbering mess. Discarded tissues were strewn around her modest room—a look she was getting used to. She didn't have the energy to pick them up and her bedroom door stayed locked all the time now. She was sick and tired of her mother barging in and complaining about the mess.

For weeks she'd felt ill, but put it down to anxiety associated with upcoming exams. She'd been studying as much as she could, but she couldn't get the queasy stomach to settle, and suffered mood swings, laughing one minute and crying uncontrollably the next. She had no idea what was wrong with her and earlier in the week, had succumbed to the need to see her family doctor, hoping he could give her something to settle it. After some routine tests Dr. Terence Scott (Scotty) called her back into the medical centre.

It was an effort to get dressed and go to see him, but she made it, although a little late for the appointment.

"Emily, how are you feeling today?" Scotty asked.

"Still the same. I feel like I'm going to be sick all the time, but when I go to do it nothing happens. I have no energy; it took me all my strength to come here. It's really frustrating and I have an exam next week, please give me something," Emily pleaded.

"Emily, I'm sorry, but there isn't anything I can give you to make you feel better, unfortunately. What you have will pass, but not for a few of months," Scotty tried to reassure her. The news had been a shock to him and he wasn't sure how she would take it. He had thought about calling in her mother, but then decided against it.

"Emily, the reason you are feeling so bad is because you are pregnant."

The look on her face told him that she was totally unaware of her condition.

"No, there must be some mistake. I haven't even had sex, so how can that be possible?" Emily asked.

Scotty could tell from her stunned expression that she firmly believed she was still a virgin.

"Emily, do you have a boyfriend, or have you been sexually active in any way?"

"No. I've only been with a boy a couple of times and we've kissed and he's played with my boobs, but nobody's ever been down there," she stated fiercely.

"You said you've never had sex, can I ask if you are taking drugs or if there is a time when you could have been drugged, because there are some drugs out there that can make you so spaced out you are not even aware of what's happening to you? Can you think of a time when something like that may have happened?"

"No, I don't think so. I . . . er, well maybe. I've dreamed about having sex. I mean, what sixteen-year-old doesn't dream about it, right? But yeah, on my sixteenth birthday I smoked a couple of joints and while I was spaced out I dreamed of it. It felt so real; do you think that could have been it?" She felt ashamed to admit the wonderful memory she had of that night. She had enjoyed it so much that it was all she ever dreamed about now.

"Yes, those dates would be about right, and if that's the only time your dream felt like it could have been real, then yes, that was probably when you conceived. Do you have any questions?" he asked.

"What do I do now?" She had no idea what she was supposed to do with this shocking piece of news.

"Well, I suppose you tell your parents that you're due to have a baby in around six months." With that, he opened the door and Emily walked out into a world that suddenly felt foreign to her.

Scotty felt sorry for the kid. She'd been through hell this last year after it was revealed that her mother Susan had been having affairs with musician Lenni Maxwell and property tycoon Grant Woodham. When Lenni was found dead at his home on the island, Susan was embroiled in the sordid mess. Although eventually cleared of all charges, the paparazzi were ruthless in their portrayal of her role in the murder case.

He could only imagine what Emily's home life was like; he knew her parents had separated. On the surface, Susan had managed to keep her real estate business going and he knew Dwayne had gone back to work at the supermarket, after recovering from his heart attack and the court case exposing his wife's affairs. Scotty noticed they chose a very low profile on the island these days.

Emily stayed with her mother after her parents separated. She wasn't proud of what her mother had done, but she had no time for her father, Dwayne: his unrealistic expectations of her were archaic. It was obvious he didn't trust anyone anymore, his daughter included. She only needed to look at someone, or be somewhere she shouldn't, and he'd go off the deep end, which for a teenager was extremely frustrating, and she wanted no part of him in her life.

There was no way she was telling her parents. No way in hell she was having that conversation with them. They would kill her. They would want to know who got her pregnant and what he was going to do about it. Hell, she didn't even know who the father was.

It was the best dream she'd ever had, the one on her sixteenth birthday, the one that felt so real, which apparently it was. In that dream she was being kissed all over from head to toe and every part in-between. The kisses were tender and loving. His hands were soft and gentle as they moved around her body and the union of their bodies made her blush as she remembered it again just now. If that was sex, then she'd definitely be doing that again; she was looking forward to it.

But who drugged her and had sex with her? She'd had a few glasses of beer with the guys from school; she shared a couple of joints with them, but she was feeling sick, and wanted to go home. She was stumbling around like she'd had too many drinks and a couple of the guys offered to walk her home, which she declined. She didn't want them to know where she was going, it was crucial nobody follow her. She didn't think they had followed her, but now she wasn't sure.

As Emily left the medical centre she kept trying to piece it all together, but nothing made any sense. How could this have happened to her? In a weird way she wanted to blame Hayley, her best friend. If Hayley hadn't ditched her six months earlier, none of this would have happened.

But now she was pregnant and, as far as she could figure out, either Zac or Lucas who offered to walk her home had indeed followed her, or could it have been Oliver? No, he'd never have done that to her. He'd never shown any signs of being interested in her that way; he was a mate, a friend.

She recalled that when she got to Oliver's house that night, the night of her sixteenth birthday, she lay down on the blanket outside because she thought she was going to be sick and didn't want to embarrass herself by doing it inside the house. She loved the feeling of being stoned; it made her forget all about the crap that was happening at her home and the stress of studying for exams. She lay there, looking up at the stars, music playing faintly in the background from somewhere. She couldn't remember much more, other than the kisses—beautiful romantic, gentle kisses all over her naked body. She remembered the lingering warmth on the rug from the afternoon sun. Had she taken her clothes off or had someone else removed them? She didn't know. She didn't recall feeling scared at any time; all she remembered was the wonderful feeling of having someone touch her in places no one had ever done before. She longed for that feeling again.

CHAPTER SEVEN

Location, Location, Location

At eight on Wednesday morning, Cameron waited patiently at the Blissful Retreat Coffee Shop for Terry to arrive for breakfast. Breakfast was normally served at the Glasstop Restaurant situated in the middle of the resort, but today it was booked out for a private function, so staff had escorted Cameron to the coffee shop, which served a more casual meal.

Cameron didn't mind, he wasn't fussy. It was going to be a busy day and he wanted something substantial in his stomach. He enjoyed toast and coffee as he waited for his eggs benedict. Terry arrived some ten minutes late.

Cameron showed him Faith's portfolio as Terry waited for his bacon and eggs to be served. Cameron reminded him they were twins, but Terry wasn't convinced they were the right look for the shoot. This made Cameron's blood boil.

"What do you mean, they don't have the right look? This is an island photo shoot. Faith and Fay live here on the island, trust me they have the right look. I'm as pissed as you that head office only sent us with one female and two male models, so we have to get talent from here anyway, at least these two have already modeled. The camera doesn't lie, they look bloody hot. They are the right look, Terry, open your bloody eyes and look at the pictures," Cameron bellowed.

"Keep your hair on. What I mean is, if we hire them, it will limit the colour scheme for the costumes, props and locations we've planned that's all."

"That's bullshit and you know it, they can wear a bloody wig, for god's sake. What's your real problem?" Cameron wasn't budging, he wanted the Ash twins, and he was going to fight for them. His memory of the previous night kept him highly motivated to get them the job.

"Sorry to interrupt Mr. Henderson, Mr. Collins. I'm Gabby Saintclaire, manager of the resort. I know we have an appointment booked in thirty minutes, but unfortunately I have just been called to an emergency, therefore I would like to introduce you to Ramon Jones, the resort photographer. He took the photos we supplied for location choices. He can also connect you with anyone else you may require to successfully achieve all that you desire while you are here on Clairemont Island. Please forgive me as I have to rush, but Ramon will look after you." Gabby ushered Ramon forward as she disappeared out of sight.

Ramon noticed the twins' portfolio; he was curious as to how they were in possession of it.

"Are you looking for models?" Ramon asked.

"Yes, we're only travelling with one female and two male models, due to a double booking," responded Cameron before Terry had a chance to answer.

"In that case, can I recommend a couple of locals who I've used over the years; I can show you their portfolios if you're interested?"

"Yes, please." Cameron glared at Terry in defiance.

"I'll go grab them. In the meantime, here are the photos of the locations you have chosen, have another look at them and we'll head out to see them when you're ready. Back in a minute."

Terry and Cameron were unanimous in approving the location selections that Ramon presented. The team at *This Could Be Your Life* magazine had spent months going through the photos, in the end deciding on the locations, with standby choices. They would see the locations today before making a final decision.

Ramon returned with six portfolios, three male and three female. He handed them to Terry and asked if they were ready to view the locations.

Fueled with a hearty breakfast, Ramon led them to the resort car which was waiting for them at the front of the resort.

Their first location was just a few minutes away along Clairemont Beach Promenade. Ramon parked toward the far end, the lighthouse in full view up a slight hill.

"I don't for one minute want to tell you how to do your job, that's not my intention. So please forgive me if I get carried away; I have photographed the island from top to bottom and from every angle imaginable. So, when I show you these locations today, I'll be explaining them from a photographer's point of view. I will, from experience, talk about the best time of the day to shoot these locations; it may just save some time as we have loads of locations to get through in a short period of time, is that OK?" Ramon hoped he wasn't overstepping the mark, but he was selling the island in the only way he knew how.

Cameron was quick to answer: "Absolutely, mate, I'm not here to reinvent the wheel, we only have a few days to photograph as much as we can; so hell, yeah, any suggestions would be greatly appreciated."

"Excellent. If you come with me, I can show you where I've taken some outstanding wedding shots incorporating the beach, the pier and the lighthouse. We are so fortunate to have the lighthouse close enough to capture shots of Clairemont Island; its beach and surrounds.

"There is limited time to shoot a sunrise, so I wonder if you've thought about setting up two sunrise shoots. One could be taken here, looking up at the lighthouse. You could have models just over there," as he pointed to a ridge in the hill about half way up. "From here, at this angle, you can get the sun rising on top of the water as it casts rays of orange hues at the base of the lighthouse, it'll look spectacular."

They walked around the beach, taking in the lighthouse as they made their way to a long wooden pier.

"If you were to set up another camera here, there aren't many yachts on this side of the pier and I've done a shot where I've placed about thirty plastic lanterns with tea lights. I've pushed them out and captured my models in a small wooden boat. Now, come over here. When the sun rises from this angle you capture the other side of the island and sometimes I've been able to get dolphins in the background. Although I can't promise that; unfortunately they don't come on cue.

The lighthouse can be shot from every angle possible— from the beach looking up at the lighthouse and from the wooden steps and from the pier. There could also be internal photos of the lighthouse's spiral staircase and vistas from the internal windows, looking out."

Terry and Cameron were speechless; the scenery was breath-taking as far as the eye could see. Ramon had described his vision in a way that even Terry could see. They were thankful Ramon was showing them around, sharing his expert opinion of locations, shots and props.

Ramon continued, "As far as beach shots, I'll give you a list of all the props I have and it will depend what background you want to incorporate; as you can see, you have plenty to choose from." His outstretched arm moved backwards to reveal the options.

"I understand you bought some outfits with you, but depending on what props you want to use, will probably depend on other clothes. I work with a couple of local designers; if you want I can arrange to drop by on our way back from seeing all the locations."

"Yes, please, that would be brilliant; it will help us to make final decisions," Terry said and Cameron nodded in agreement.

Ramon made the calls as Terry and Cameron made their way up to the lighthouse. From the top of the hill, the view of the island was impeccable.

"Oh, and see that yacht over there, moored over by the heads, the big white one? That's your next location. I can't take you on-board today, but we will have a crew to take care of us while we sail around Clairemont Island for a sunset cruise. Drinks and nibbles have been provided by the owner on the proviso we don't trash his prized possession."

"Wow, she's a beauty. That's going to be one hell of a photo shoot." Terry couldn't believe his eyes. "Who's the owner?" he asked.

"The owner is none other than the mayor of Clairemont Island, Denzel Woods. He and his wife Sabrina own Clairemont supermarket, the medical centre and a few other buildings. They're in Hong Kong at the moment; otherwise I know they'd be on board to welcome you. But the crew knows what they're doing; there have been hundreds of parties on board that yacht."

Ramon parked in the guest car park of Grandberry Estate. "This is a three hundred acre privately owned family estate that has bred thoroughbred horses for over fifty years;

they've done very well for themselves. The winery was introduced to the estate about twenty years ago when the adjoining property went into receivership, and more recently, due to new blood in the family, they spent a few million dollars building a health spa, and a quaint chapel. Also, they renovated one of the stables to incorporate a function centre as well as upgrading their restaurant to cater to the wedding market. They've kept the original theme and feel of old cobblestone buildings. Grandberry Estate has been featured in quite a few magazines."

The immaculate attention to detail of each building took Cameron's eye immediately. "It looks like each stone on the building has been polished clean, and the cobblestones on the ground they're as clean as a whistle, do they not bring horses or cars through this area?" Cameron asked.

"Yes, they do, I have no idea how they do it, but I totally agree, it looks like this every time I've come here." He too was baffled as to how they could keep everything immaculate and pristine.

They lost themselves in thought as they meandered through the estate. Cameron looked at each detail as if through the lens of a camera.

"As you can see by walking through to the many buildings, the gardens that connect the buildings are simply divine. You have certainly come at the most perfect time of the year. This private garden is not open to the public; only guests get to see this majestic display of flora." Cameron stood to take in the magnificence of the ocean of purple, mauve and white wisteria cascading down over the many ponds and water features. Around further, a man-made lake was swamped with mass plantings of lavender.

"They also have a couple of carriages we can use for some horse and carriage shots. I've done that before. They had an old Clydesdale they hitched up to an open carriage, which I used for a wedding a few years back. Not sure they still have that horse, but they have plenty of other horses to choose from, they're very accommodating.

"Now, let's walk through the health and wellness retreat on our way to the winery, I've got some ideas you may like to think about." Ramon was willing to offer as many suggestions as he could, but at the end of the day he knew it was their choice.

They walked the long way around to the winery, taking in the seductive and intoxicating smell of jasmine that lingered through the Zen-inspired Japanese retreat. Soft seductive music played in the background as they casually strolled amongst the ever colourful nandina and perfectly manicured bright green shrubs surrounding seated areas. It was an area you felt compelled to sit, relax and absorb the ambience. There was so much to see in this small but inviting space. Quaint concrete statues dotted amongst shrubs and traditional warriors guarding the entrance made the garden feel safe and serene.

At the edge of the property Cameron stood taking in the view. The long lines of grape vines stretched for miles.

He counted what looked like ten villas and noticed the cobblestone theme continue throughout the winery. Each villa had an uninterrupted view of the rolling rows of grape vines. To the left, Cameron could make out the man-made lake of Grandberry Estate, and to the right, a mountain range.

"The cellar door has the best Italian gourmet pizza on the island, the pasta is really good too, and they offer wine tasting seven days a week. For that front cover photo, if you stand here as the sun sets, with all the lights on inside the winery and function centre, you get an explosion of yellows and oranges with a tinge of red. Totally spectacular, like nothing you've ever seen before." Ramon's passion was evident.

"I don't know what to say, this place is outstanding, I'm so grateful to have the opportunity to shoot in such a beautiful location. Who knew there was so much to see on such a small island?" Terry stated the obvious.

"That's why I love the island, I wouldn't dream of leaving; it's the best place in the world, as far as I'm concerned," Ramon replied.

"The next location is again a private garden, much smaller in comparison and owned by a lovely old lady. Unfortunately, she's in a nursing home now, but her cottage and garden have been heritage listed and the heritage society makes sure the building and grounds are kept in immaculate condition. Volunteers work all year round to keep it looking the way it does. Used mostly for weddings these days.

"It's about a ten-minute drive from here as I have to stop to pick up the key, which won't take long. The cottage is still furnished and some of the rooms are OK to shoot in, but lighting is a real pain. I tend not to shoot inside, but of course that will be your call."

As Ramon parked to get the key, Cameron was the first to speak: "He may be an outstanding photographer, but the photos we had sent to us pale in comparison to what we've seen today, don't you think?"

"I have to agree. I haven't looked through your eyes, but what I've seen today is bloody amazing," Terry concurred.

From the road there was no visible sign of what was to become an explosion of colour. The brilliant display of greens, reds, yellows, browns and all colours in between, mass planted around a delightful cobblestone cottage. Behind the cottage a leisurely stream weaved its way to a large pond with red painted arch bridges, beckoning you to continue exploring.

They walked around the pond taking in the secluded areas where park benches, tables, chairs and love seats were strategically placed for prime photo shoots; it truly was a magnificent setting.

Cameron and Terry agreed with Ramon about the inside of the cottage—although delightful in its own way, it just wasn't right for this photo shoot. The gardens, on the other hand, were perfect.

"Ramon, I reckon we've seen enough, I don't think we need to see the other locations. What do you think Terry?" Cameron asked.

"I agree. If you can take us back to the resort, we've still got heaps to do before our crew meeting at 5:00 p.m." Terry said.

"Don't forget, we're stopping in to see both designers on the way back, but that shouldn't take long," Ramon reminded them.

"Terry and Cameron, this is Michelle Perry, one of our many talented designers on the island. Michelle specialises in after five and evening wear. I'm sure there will be something here that'll be perfect for the sunset yacht cruise." Ramon took a seat as he left them to go through the many racks of designer clothes.

Neither Terry nor Cameron had looked at the portfolios Ramon had given to them earlier, but Michelle assured them that she had dressed all the models on the island at one time or another so she would have something they could wear. All they had to do was let her know by 5:00 p.m. which models they were using and she'd bring an assortment of clothes to the relevant locations.

Their last stop was to meet designer Bree Dominic, owner of Klassy Klozit: Specializing in sleek, modern and funky fashion.

"Bree dresses a lot of my models; she's got a great eye and I'm sure she'll have what you're looking for." Ramon introduced them and sat quietly reading the paper as he waited for them to finish choosing the necessary outfits.

Back at the resort, Ramon led them to the meeting room; he grabbed some sandwiches and drinks then left them to it as he went to get the props list.

Fifteen minutes later, Ramon walked into a heated argument between Terry and Cameron; they were arguing over the Ash twins. It seemed that Terry didn't want to hire them for the shoot. Ramon didn't understand—the twins were fantastic to work for, could wear anything and, to top it off, the camera loved them. Riffling through paperwork, Ramon decided it best to stay out of the way as it had nothing to do with him.

"This is bullshit. You're blind as a bat if you can't see that they're perfect. Look, Terry, look the camera doesn't lie—so what's your bloody problem?" Cameron demanded.

"I think we can do better. Here, look at this one. Lucy, she's a knockout, she will work in well with Molly, Robbie and Brenton, she's all we need. It's Lucy or none." Terry wasn't budging.

"I'm the photographer, I say who the models are, and I say what they wear and which shoot they're on. It has nothing to do with you. I'm not even sure why I'm having this conversation with you. I'm hiring the twins, end of story." Cameron spat the words with a vengeance.

"Oh yes, it does. I'm the public relations and project manager, I call the shots and it's Lucy. We'll pair her up with Robbie; they'll look sensational together." For a minute Terry thought he had won.

Ramon interrupted: "Tell you what, why don't I call Lucy and see if she's available for the shoot dates and times; have you finalised the call sheet yet?" Ramon asked as he picked up his phone to dial Lucy.

"I've almost finished the call sheet. We are just working on the models and costumes. All locations are locked in and we've decided to do the sunset shoot at the vineyard, so give me a minute to update that now and you can let Lucy know dates and times for each shoot." Terry frantically punched the keys of the laptop as he spoke.

While Ramon called Lucy, Cameron looked over the props list. Head down scanning the pages, he was thankful for the distraction.

"I swear to God, I'm going to have the twins on this shoot if it's the last thing I do," Cameron muttered under his breath.

"Hello, Lucy, it's Ramon. Not sure you're aware that there's a magazine doing a photo shoot over the next few days. I hope you don't mind, but I gave them your portfolio and they want you as one of their models. Would you be available for a sunrise shoot tomorrow, 4:00 a.m. till 11:00 a.m.? The following day, it's a sunset shoot 3:00 p.m. till 10:00 p.m., then an 8:00 a.m. – 8:00 p.m. with a break in the middle of the day, then two nine to five days."

Ramon sat with fingers crossed. He had great respect for Lucy, she was drop dead gorgeous, great fun to be around and wonderful to work with, but he'd heard on the grapevine that she was no longer interested in doing this sort of thing anymore. Since she'd started living with Troy, her focus had changed; she was intent on building a life with Troy, and no longer looking to fulfil her dream of leaving the island. Well, that's what he'd heard. He knew Troy had proposed to her a few weeks ago—he'd helped Troy dress the bedroom, but hadn't heard if she'd accepted or not. He believed no news was good news, and he hoped it was: they were a great couple.

"Ramon, it's a real honour to be chosen, but I don't know, my head's in another place now. I know I used to love modeling, but it's just not my thing anymore. Are you sure they really want me? What about the twins or Ella, or some of the other girls? There's plenty of talent on the island, I'm sure they'd be better than me."

"Lucy, they want you."

"Can I think about it? I'd have to change some of my shifts at the resort, and at this short notice I'm not sure they'd let me have tomorrow off." Lucy was intrigued, to say the least.

"Tell you what, Lucy, think about it for a few minutes, talk to Troy, ask if you can get the time off and get back to me within the hour, OK?" Ramon wondered if she was scared to tell Troy. After all, this kind of thing was her old life, pre-Troy, but he could be wrong, she may just have been taken by surprise.

While Ramon waited for Lucy to call back, he started working with Cameron on the props list. Terry had gone for a walk to clear his head. Together Cameron and Ramon finalised the call sheet, all apart from the last model. Front reception was photocopying everything ready for the crew meeting at 5:00 p.m. The clothing list was faxed off to the necessary boutiques. That wouldn't change, the twins and Lucy were the same size, so it wouldn't matter who wore the outfits.

Ramon suggested a drink at the bar, it had been a full on day and he thought they could take a few minutes to catch their breath. He also wanted to find out what was going on between Terry and Cameron, and a couple of beers might just open him up to talk.

Once they were seated in the Zanzabar, Andrew served them beers. Andrew remembered Cameron from the night before. "How was your location scouting, did we manage to impress you?" Andrew asked.

"Hell yeah, what a stunningly beautiful island you have here. I've travelled extensively and photographed in some of the most exotic countries of the world, but I have never seen anything quite so beautiful as what I've seen today." Cameron's tone and expression changed as he talked about the island.

Ramon thanked Andrew; he'd noticed the change and wanted to start Cameron on another conversation.

"Hey, I'm a bit confused about why Terry doesn't want the twins, what's the story there?

"I've no idea; he's a friggin' idiot, that's what. I've just about had enough of him interfering in my work. I wish to hell he'd never come. We don't need him, I could have organized everything for the shoot," Cameron stated.

"But he is the project manager; therefore I imagine he will have to OK the talent. I gather that's what he's here for, and to make sure all the legals fall within the guidelines of company policy?" Ramon cautiously replied.

"He doesn't care about following company policy; he's proved that more than once already on this trip. If he doesn't stay out of my way, I'll dob the prick into head office."

Just as Ramon was going to interject, they were interrupted. The crew was arriving for their 5:00 p.m. meeting.

"Grab yourselves a drink and I'll take you through to the meeting room," Ramon told the crew.

As Ramon was escorting the crew to the meeting room, Lucy called.

"Hey Ramon, I've given this some thought and I'm not going to go ahead with the shoot. Please thank them for thinking of me, but I'm just not into it anymore."

"Cameron, can I have a moment before you go into the crew meeting?" Ramon asked.

"Sure thing, what's up?"

"Lucy just called to say she's thankful for the opportunity, but has said no. Sorry about that." Ramon wondered what the outcome of that conversation would be.

Cameron thought about what to do next, and then decided to do nothing. He didn't tell Terry that Lucy had declined the offer; instead he said it was all arranged and led Terry to believe that Lucy was on board. He excused himself from the meeting to make the call to Faith and set the twins up for the shoot in the morning.

The twins were ecstatic, but Cameron asked them to keep it to themselves for now. He arranged to meet with them later that night, for some fun.

The crew was given their call sheets for the five days. They talked through their roles, partners, costumes and props for each shoot. After the two-hour meeting, they each went their own way, some electing to head back to the bar.

For the third time, Cameron tried to call his fiancée, Anthea, but she wasn't answering her mobile or their Los Angeles landline, which annoyed him even more. Where was she? Why wasn't she at home at two in the morning? Was she really having an affair on him? Who was the man she'd embraced outside the restaurant? Why had he kissed her? Her deception was eating away at him.

Cameron took the short stroll down to the esplanade where he was to meet the twins. Cameron was looking forward to an evening with them—he could still taste them, and the swelling in his pants sent a shiver down his spine in anticipation. As he walked up to the Irish pub he could see them sitting outside, they were talking to some young guys, who moved on when Cameron walked closer.

"Friends of yours?" Cameron asked.

"Yeah, we've known each other for years. They were inviting us to a party tonight, but we weren't sure it would be your thing, even though you seemed to enjoy yourself last night. I reckon they'll have the same stash if not something way better, if you're up to it?" Faith hoped like hell he was; she was hanging out for a hit, she'd had a hell of a day.

"Bring it on. I'm up for whatever you want to throw at me." Cameron had never been so open before. Tonight he was going to throw caution to the wind, have a great time and accept whatever happened.

They ate dinner at the Irish pub, and then walked to the party; it was only a block away. Faith knew she would get wasted and didn't want the temptation of driving home afterwards; hopefully they'd all end up back at Cameron's room at the resort and continue where they left off the night before.

They knew they had a 4:00 a.m. shoot and they should be responsible and all that crap, but Cameron just didn't care; he wanted to numb his brain, forget that Anthea existed. He wanted to get wasted and that's just what he did. All three of them drank shots of whiskey and snorted so much coke, it was a wonder they didn't fry their brains.

At 1:00 a.m. they staggered back to the resort where they made love till the alarm went off at 3:30 a.m. The cold shower didn't do much to bring them back to normality, but they turned up outside the resort and filed into the minibus van to take them to the lighthouse.

CHAPTER EIGHT

Dirty Little Secrets

Dwayne Olsen was not happy; he'd never fully recovered since his heart attack the previous year. It was during his recovery that he learned his wife Susan had been having affairs with both Lenni Maxwell and Grant Woodham. He kind of knew something wasn't right with their relationship, but to learn of not just one affair but a double whammy was almost more than he could bear. Eighteen years of marriage slipped away amidst a brutally public court case where justice was finally served, and Grant Woodham was sentenced to ten years for the involuntary manslaughter of Lenni Maxwell.

Anger and hatred toward Susan didn't account for much as his private life was uncovered for all to ridicule. He battled through the court case mainly to support his fifteen-year-old daughter Emily—not that their relationship was close, it hadn't been for years. In truth, his focus had drifted away from his family, probably around the same time he started coaching the local footy team—something he was more passionate about at that time. On reflection, he wondered if he had caused the distance between them all, or if it had already started to occur and, unconsciously, he had just gone with the flow.

After the court case, when Susan was cleared of involvement in Lenni's murder, Dwayne took a month off work and made some serious life decisions. He opted to stay on the island and keep his job, but he did let go of the coaching. He didn't want to put any more pressure on his heart: it had well and truly suffered enough so he wasn't game to tempt fate too much. He moved into his own one-bedroom apartment on the island, and proceeded to get on with life.

Kathy O'Connell shared his office space at the Clairemont Supermarket; they had worked together for the last twenty years. He was the bookkeeper and Kathy the admin officer for the supermarket. Kathy had been dealt the unfortunate task of telling Dwayne that Susan was having an affair with Lenni Maxwell. Nobody at that point knew of her additional affair with Grant Woodham, so when that came out Kathy was very concerned for Dwayne's overall health. Over this year, though, he seemed to have mellowed out, but she knew he didn't enjoy his job anymore. He never talked about his private life, not even to Kathy or Simon her husband, and they had been friends since school, so she had no idea what he did with himself when he left the office each day.

Kathy watched as Dwayne pounded away at his calculator. He had a kind, generous nature and a beautiful smile, but she hadn't seen that side of him for quite some time. It was when Dwayne's mobile rang, that his face turned a deathly shade of white. He looked at the number, slumped his shoulders in defeat. Kathy didn't know who was calling but she could tell it wasn't someone Dwayne wanted to talk to. She could tell he was debating whether to answer it.

It was his wife, Susan. He had no idea why she would call him at work, they hadn't spoken in almost a year. In truth he didn't want to speak to her ever again, but after the tenth ring he realised she wasn't going away. He reluctantly answered.

"What do you want?" he gruffly responded.

"You need to come here now; something has happened that you need to know about." Susan was none too happy making the call, but she had no idea what she was supposed to do.

"I'll come around after work," Dwayne replied.

NO! Now. You need to come now," Susan said as she slammed the phone down.

Kathy knew this was not a good sign, she asked Dwayne if he was OK. Dwayne reassured her he was, he'd had a clean bill of health from the medical team looking after him, but he certainly was not happy with this phone call or the prospect of having to see Susan again.

He picked up his keys, slammed the office door shut and drove the short distance to his home, the marital home where he had spent many happy years. He had walked out of his home a year earlier, vowing never to return.

Without thinking, he walked in the front door. He didn't knock—he was past caring about what he was technically supposed to do.

Susan and his daughter, Emily, were seated at opposite ends of the kitchen table, neither was smiling and you could have cut the air with a knife, the tension was so thick.

"Well, what do you need me for?" Dwayne wasn't interested in their bickering. He felt like being sick, this house started clawing at his skin the minute he walked in.

"Seems your daughter has gotten herself pregnant, and she won't tell me who the father is." Susan was furious.

"Well, look at the example you're setting. Maybe if you were home once in a while instead of screwing everything in town, you may notice what your daughter is up to." Dwayne spat the words with a vengeance.

"Maybe if you showed some interest in your daughter she might not have gotten in this mess," Susan lashed back.

Emily felt sick, really sick. She tried to leave the table, but was quickly dragged back to her seat. "You are not leaving that seat until you tell us who did this to you." Susan wasn't letting her away that easily.

"I told you. I don't know."

"What are you saying?" Dwayne asked. "Are you saying that you've had sex with that many boys you don't know which one is the father?"

"No, I'm not saying that at all. I'm saying that I didn't even know I'd had sex, someone drugged me," Emily tried to defend herself.

"Well then, you need to go to a doctor for tests. Take her to the doctor, Susan; find out what's going on," Dwayne demanded.

"She's already been to the doctor, he's taken tests, and she's pregnant, due in six months."

"Emily, who are you hanging around with who feels they have to drug you to have sex, and where did they get drugs from? Are you taking drugs?" Dwayne looked at her with disgust.

Who drugged her? That was the million-dollar question she'd been asking herself that question for days now. She must be very careful in her response; she mustn't put herself in danger. After all, she was supplying drugs to her friends at school, and it may have been because of these drugs she got pregnant. She must never mention Oliver; he's the best thing that's ever happened to her. Her response was to stay quietly tight-lipped.

"Emily! I'm speaking to you! Who did this to you? her father screamed at her.

"I don't know," she screamed back.

"Give me your phone. Go to your room and stay there, you are not leaving this house until we get some answers, do you understand?" Susan grabbed Emily's mobile phone.

Sifting through her recent calls, messages and Facebook page, there was nothing out of the ordinary. Just messages to and from Hayley, which was normal, and the conversation was all about school, exams and a guy called Josh who Hayley seemed to be involved with, but nothing unusual to warrant concern.

"I have to get back to work. Let's just sit on this for a while, see what plays out. I might do some investigating myself. I'll ring you in a couple of days to see what's happening. Is that OK?" Dwayne asked Susan.

"Yeah, I'd like that." Susan felt reassured; she was reminded of a time long ago when Dwayne used to be like this, authoritative and in control. That was when she loved him—before he became the pathetic shell of a man he was now. Seeing this glimmer of the man she once loved made her wonder if they could ever rebuild the past. Would there, could there ever be a future for them again as man and wife, or had she completely killed their relationship?

The next day after school, Dwayne was seated in a coffee shop waiting for a glimpse of his daughter as she left the school grounds. At first, he just wanted to see who she was hanging out with. As she said her goodbyes to a small group of girls, she started walking in the opposite direction from her home. Curious, Dwayne decided to follow her. Thankfully, Emily would never expect to see her father out of his office at this time of the day; chances were she wouldn't notice him.

From the other side of the road and quite some distance behind her, Dwayne followed his daughter to a modest looking weatherboard on the outskirts of town. He had no idea who lived in the house; he didn't think he'd ever been up this end of town before.

He found a shady spot on the other side of the street, with a direct view of the front of the house. He hoped he was far enough back, so that when she came out, she wouldn't see him. At 6:30 p.m. she emerged from the house dressed in a flimsy summer dress. She had her school backpack draped over her left shoulder and walked back into town with a swing in her step.

What had she been doing inside that house for three hours? It wasn't Hayley's house: Hayley was with the group of girls Emily had said goodbye to at the school gate. Did Emily have a boyfriend after all?

Dwayne pondered what to do next, should he knock on the door and see who answered, but then what would he say? Are you the one who knocked my daughter up? What are you going to do about it? What if his parents answered? He needed to think about how he was going to verbalise the fact their son drugged, raped and then got Emily pregnant. He needed to give this more thought, he might only get one chance, and he couldn't just barge on in with all guns blazing.

He was just about to leave when he noticed a couple of young girls knock on the door. It was answered, they talked for a bit and then left.

Then the door opened and a middle-aged, longhaired gangly man walked out. Dwayne thought this must be the kid's father; he wondered where the man was going at this time of the night. Dwayne crossed the road and followed the man down to Clairemont pier, where he boarded the ferry.

Dwayne spent the rest of the night debating what to do next. Should he speak to Emily and say he'd followed her? Should he go to the house and confront the family about what their son had done? Or should he forget it and carry on with his miserable life. Susan had made it abundantly clear she wanted nothing to do with him and, to be honest, the sight of her made him sick. He'd stopped being a part of their daughter's life well before he found out Susan was having an affair, so he felt comfortable enough to walk away and leave it up to them to sort out. By the time he curled up into bed he had decided it was no longer his problem, he had been outcast from his family for over a year. Now, as he welcomed sleep, he comfortably relinquished any further involvement in their problems.

What he was not expecting was the guilt-ridden dreams that tormented his sleep. Tossing and turning he was inundated with bodies having sex with this daughter. At one point he even thought that he too had sex with her; the thought repulsed him. He woke shaking uncontrollably. Trying to get the thoughts from his mind, he reached for the bottle of Bourbon beside his bed, poured half a glass, and attempted to make sense of his dreams.

He thought maybe he wasn't ready to accept that someone could drug and rape his daughter. He knew he had to find out who was responsible; they had to pay for what they did.

Next day, again at 3:00 p.m., he sat waiting, watching as Emily came out of the school gates. Once again, she waved goodbye to her friends and walked to the outskirts of town, once again she went inside the same house.

Once again, Dwayne settled himself in the shady spot opposite the house.

About ten minutes later, that same middle-aged man, dressed in jeans and sleeveless shirt, his arms covered in tribal tattoos, walked up to the house. He opened the door and walked inside.

Dwayne waited another thirty minutes, and then walked over to the front door, hesitated for only a minute then knocked.

"Hello, can I help you?" asked the middle-aged, longhaired, gangly man with a scar that ran the length of his face from the corner of his eye to his jawline. Up close, the sight of him almost took Dwayne's breath away.

"Hello, I . . . er . . . need to speak to your son, please," Dwayne fumbled over his words; this was way more intimidating than he'd rehearsed.

"I don't have a son, what makes you think I do?" Oliver replied.

"Then who lives here with you?" Dwayne was starting to panic.

"Nobody, I live here by myself. Why do you want to know?" Oliver had already given more information than he felt comfortable with.

"My name is Dwayne Olsen, I am Emily's father. I saw her come in here, what is she doing here with you?" For the first time ever, Dwayne started to hyperventilate.

"Hey, you OK? You don't look too good. Come on in, I'll get you some water." Oliver opened the door and Dwayne hesitantly made his way inside.

There she was, headphones on, sitting on the sofa, playing the PlayStation.

She looked up as her father entered the house.

"What are you doing here?" she demanded to know.

"I followed you, that's what. If you aren't going to tell us who got you pregnant, then I have a duty of care to find out for myself.

Oliver looked at Emily. "What, you're pregnant? When did this happen? Why didn't you tell me?" The shocked look on his face led Dwayne to believe this was the first time he'd heard of it.

Dwayne looked back at Oliver: "Who are you and what is Emily doing here?" This whole scenario just didn't feel right to him.

"My name is Oliver and I met Emily about six months ago. She was in a really bad way as a result of your separation and school exams. She started coming here just to get away from all the aggravation. She comes over whenever she wants, lets herself in, plugs in the PlayStation and loses herself in that for hours at a time. That's all, nothing else. Trust me, I haven't laid a finger on her."

"This is not right." Dwayne was struggling to understand what was going on. "Come on Emily, I'm taking you home and you are never to come back here again. Do you understand me? This is wrong on so many levels."

"You should be ashamed of yourself, encouraging a young girl into your home. She's too young to understand the dangers of this, but you should know better." Dwayne spat the words as he dragged an uncooperative Emily out the door.

On the footpath outside Oliver's home Emily screamed at Dwayne: "You are wrong about him, he's my friend, he's the only one who listens to me, who cares about me. You don't care about me, and Mum only thinks of herself. Oliver is always there for me, he talks to me, asks about my day, cooks me tea and helps me with my homework. When was the last time you did any of that? Never! That's when. Mum spends all day and night at work and drinks till she passes out."

"Emily, that's enough. When have you ever allowed us the opportunity to do that for you? You shut us out well before we separated, and you know that. Don't you see how wrong this is? Hell, he's my age, he should know better than to encourage you?" Dwayne was struggling to comprehend what was happening.

"I don't care what you say, I'm going to stay with Oliver, Mum is miserable all the time and I don't want to be around her, or you." Emily pulled herself free from her father's tight grip and ran back to Oliver's front door, pulled out her key, opened the door and slammed it shut, leaving Dwayne bewildered.

How on earth had this happened? His sixteen-year-old daughter was virtually living with a man old enough to be her father; she comes and goes as she pleases, she has her own key to his house. She considers him to be her friend. What's really going on inside that house?

Dwayne had heard what Oliver said, but every ounce of his fibre told him a different story, one filled with a more sinister interpretation.

He knew he had to talk to Susan about this, but he didn't want to—he wasn't sure he could contain his anger toward her, especially now. He blamed her for all of this. If she'd been faithful, Emily would not have needed to find somewhere else to go to feel wanted. Yes, it was all Susan's fault.

As he went back to his apartment, he noticed Troy lock up his new law office and start to walk home. He fell into step with him.

"Hey, mate, how's everything with you?" Troy asked.

"Are you in a hurry to get home, I'd love to buy you a drink?" Dwayne had great respect for Troy.

"Problem?" Troy enquired.

"Yeah, I think so."

"Then by all means, let's grab a drink." Troy ushered him into the Irish pub where they made their way to the back of the bar, away from the dinner crowd.

"What's up?" Troy asked as Dwayne placed their drinks on the table. Dwayne explained what unfolded at Oliver's home earlier that evening.

"I honestly don't know what to do next. If some young punk has done this to Emily, then how do we prove that Emily didn't consent to it, will a court case do any good or just tarnish her reputation? What about the kid that did this, will this ruin his chances in life, and what will it do to his family? I mean, ours is already destroyed, why ruin another family? I have a real uneasy feeling about this guy Oliver; you should have seen him, evil as sin. What if he's been grooming her, she's been going there for six months, and she's almost living there with him. I'm torn between making the bastard pay, which he should, but then I don't want to drag Emily through the court system; we both know what that does to your self-esteem. She's only a kid. Please tell me there is something I can do which doesn't drag Emily through the papers and portray her as a slut." Dwayne was desperate.

"Look, there are many things we can do, but unfortunately, yes, if you want to take this further, then it will most probably result in a court case, unless they want to settle out of court and you never know, they may. It will depend on just how much they will lose in the long run, and how something like this will damage their reputation. But we do need to know who the father is before we can go any further.

"How do I find out more about this guy Oliver?" Dwayne asked.

"Not sure, I can't say I've ever heard of him. What does he look like?" Troy asked.

"Trust me, you would never forget him. He's got to be fifty something, tall, gangly, with long hair and a scar running the length of his face, from the corner of his eye to his jaw, there is no forgetting that face."

"Then, no, can't say that I've had the pleasure," Troy responded.

"Hey, thanks for listening. I can't say I feel any better—my gut is fair churning, but at least I'm not as angry as I was. I'll pop into your office if I uncover anything else. I'd rather talk to you than Katrina. I know she's lovely and really good at her job, but reckon once I mention this to her, all hell will break loose."

"You may be right. I'm happy to talk through different scenarios, but remember to keep it all in perspective and don't go doing anything stupid, OK!"

"Yeah, got ya. It's just between us. I'm not even going to mention this to Susan." Dwayne felt more in control now that he'd spoken to someone about it, and he trusted Troy. Troy had defended Grant Woodham at Lenni's trial and Grant was sentenced to ten years for his part in the murder. With parole, he'd be out in fewer than seven, but he's in prison and Susan lost both the men she was having affairs with—to Dwayne that was sweet revenge.

Troy walked in through the front door to be met with the aromatic smell of garlic and something he couldn't quite detect.

"Hey beautiful, I'm home."

"Perfect timing. I'm in the kitchen; I was just getting dinner out of the oven. It's garlic lobster in coconut jasmine rice. How come you're late, did you get a client?" Lucy asked.

"No, but I did get stopped by Dwayne Olsen on the way home, he wanted to chat so we stopped off at the pub for a drink."

"Gosh I haven't seen him in ages; actually, I don't think I've seen him since the court case finished. Is he OK?" Lucy asked. She liked Dwayne. She was impressed with the way he held himself together during the trial, especially when he found out what his wife had been up to.

"Not sure he'll ever be OK; seems his life just keeps crumbling around him. Remember his daughter Emily? Well it seems she was drugged, raped and is now pregnant. She won't tell them who the father is and Dwayne followed her from school to find out she's been living with some old guy. He doesn't know what to do., He's too scared to go to the police because then it will get investigated and Emily will be hung out to dry for the whole town to see, and what good is that going to do her? He's also worried about the young kid who got her pregnant, what will happen to him? Poor bugger,

I feel sorry for him, seems he can't get a break."

"How old is she? I thought she was really young. She didn't seem that old the couple of days she was in the court room?" Lucy asked.

"I think he said she was sixteen."

"What do you mean, she's been living with someone, who? Is she not living with Susan anymore?"

"No, Dwayne said it was an old guy, some evil looking dude with a scar down his face. I haven't seen anyone around like that, have you?"

Lucy took a mouthful of food; she slowly chewed before answering: "I forgot to mention that Ramon called to ask if I wanted to do a photo shoot for a magazine company that's here. I said no, but I was thrilled to be asked," Lucy excitedly announced.

"What did you say no for? You always liked doing that kind of thing with Ramon; it would be good for you." Troy was curious about her response.

"Na, not anymore. That was my old life."

"Please don't think that because of me you can't do it; honestly, I'm OK with you doing whatever makes you happy. If you want to do it, please go ahead." Troy would do anything to make her happy, he loved her so much, and he was patiently waiting for the answer to his proposal. He didn't want to hassle her to make a decision, but he wondered why it was taking so long to decide if she wanted to spend the rest of her life with him.

After dinner, Lucy excused herself saying she needed to pop out and get some groceries. Troy was busy working in his office at home so she knew he wouldn't miss her, and she would be really quick, thirty minutes tops. Hell, Troy wouldn't even realise she'd gone out.

Thirty minutes passed and she still hadn't plucked up the courage to get out of her car; she knew she had to confront him again but was scared to death to broach the subject. Just thinking of it sent shivers down her spine.

Eventually she approached his front door. She knocked and waited, her heart pounding so loudly she could hardly hear herself think. As he answered, her gut instinct was to run, to get away, and to leave the island once and for all.

"Ah Lucy, I knew you'd come crawling back. I knew my magnetic charm would bring you back to me eventually."

"Don't flatter yourself, Oliver. I'm here to warn you to stay away from Emily, or else I'll be forced to tell her the truth about you. If I find out she's still hanging around, I'll go to the authorities," Lucy warned.

"Watch what you wish for Lucy. You are beautiful, but I can certainly change your appearance, and then see if the lawyer hangs around," he whispered in her ear.

Lucy ran to her car, parked at the beach, sat on the warm sand and cried until there were no tears left. She knew the only way to be free was to get him out of her life once and for all, but how? If she went to the authorities then her dirty little secret would come out and that was what she feared the most. She had to find another way; time was running out.

She stopped at the supermarket, grabbed some bread, milk and toiletries and then made her way back home to Troy, to her sanctuary, her haven.

CHAPTER NINE

Photo Shoot Day 1

As the crew boarded the two minivans to drive the short distance to the beach, totally preoccupied getting everything into the vans, they didn't notice the twins sitting in the back amongst the clothes and paraphernalia. It wasn't until they'd parked at the beach, as close as they could to the lighthouse, that they started piling out of the van. It was then that Terry saw them.

"What in the hell are they doing here? I told you I wanted Lucy on the shoot, not them," Terry shouted.

"I told you, this is my shoot. I'm in charge of who I hire, and I want them; they have the perfect look, and if you pulled your head out of your arse you'd see that." Cameron tried his best to remain calm.

"Just know that I'm seriously considering informing head office of what's just happened. You know I'm in charge on this shoot, I make the decisions and you'd better start following orders." Terry was adamant.

"Terry, you can jam it where it best fits. I have no intention of following your orders. You know jack shit about what happens on a photo shoot—you come out of your corner office thinking you know how it all runs down here in the real world, which you don't, so sit down, shut up and let me do what I've done all my life, take award winning photos. OK!" A riled Cameron walked away before his fist hit its target.

"Katy, I want Molly ready to go first. She's to be dressed in the white Chanel we brought with us, use the short black wig, the bob style, check to see if we have a long piece of white organza silk to drape around her shoulders. Molly has the solo beach shoot position 1. I want Faith and Robbie dressed in the wedding outfits for the lighthouse shoot position 2, use the white lace one. Bree will drop off her outfits within the hour.

"Then I want Fay and Brenton dressed in the blue and white outfits for the pier shoot position 3. Any problems? No! Good. Work together, guys, we don't have much time. I want to make the most out of our golden hour which will be position 3 at the pier."

Totally ignoring Terry, he went down to the beach to make sure the strobe and lights were set up in the correct position for Molly's shoot. Anton, his assistant had everything under control.

He then made his way to the next position, which was halfway up the hill to the lighthouse; this would give him an uninterrupted view of the models, the lighthouse just beyond them and the rays of sun rising. It would be stunning. He set his mark and continued walking to the final location, which was at the base of the pier.

The pier took much longer to secure the shooting position; he wanted to capture all four elements, the models, the lighthouse, the pier and the lit lanterns bobbing in the water in the one composition. After a few minutes of talking to

Anton, Stefan and Lucas he made the judgment call, that this would be shot from three different angles.

He would put Fay and Brenton in the small white canoe, place the lit lanterns around the boat, and follow them as they slowly made their way toward the pier.

He directed Stefan and Lucas, the lighting technicians, to implement his vision. He also decided to move some of the lanterns further down the beach to backdrop Molly's shoot.

Cameron returned to the tent the crew had set up on the beach to provide privacy and shelter from the sun.

Melody was his preferred stylist; she'd worked with him for many years. They had the same style sense which made it so much easier on shoots like this, where he needed to focus all of his time on taking photos and not worry about the models. The effects of the night before were starting to take its toll on him; he was in desperate need of coffee.

Melody had just finished dressing Molly as Cameron walked into the tent. "You look amazing, Molly. Give me five minutes to have a coffee and we'll go down and start."

As Cameron drank his coffee and nibbled on a croissant, he checked the progress of the models. Makeup artist/hair stylist Katy Pringle was giving Faith sexy, smoky eyes. Melody was about to dress Robbie. Giving Faith a secret wink and thumbs up, he checked the laptop for updates of the correct sunrise position; he walked back down to the beach, made final adjustments to the camera Anton had set up, and waited for Molly to join him.

Moments later, Molly was standing on cue. "Excellent, we've got the organza silk drape. Molly, what I want you to do is to slowly turn around and around, hold the drape in both hands. Then, as you're turning, hold the drape up to catch any breeze, but keep the drape at arm's length, so it's flying out from behind you. I want to catch the stages of the sun as it begins to rise, the white gown on the dark sand and black water will look stunning as the white, red and golden tones reflect in the drape."

"Like this?" Molly asked as she tried to turn around and around, nearly falling as she tripped over her feet.

"Yes, but we'll ditch the shoes; bare feet will work best. Now try."

"That's so much easier. Is this what you want?" Molly was doing exactly what he wanted.

Cameron adjusted his camera as the first signs of the rising sun appeared over the black ocean.

"Keep doing that, Molly. I want just a bit more orange in the background; give me a few more twirls."

"OK, done. Now can I get you to turn and face the ocean? Walk to camera left slightly. OK, now stop! Now arch your back just a little. Yeah, that's it, perfect. Look at me, great, chin down, more, more, stay there, and don't move. Anton, can you please turn on the fan, I want to get the drape to blow up slightly, not too high, just hip height. OK, perfect, that's a wrap for this position."

He was thrilled with the way the rays of orange kissed the back of her waist, the contrast of colours as the waves lapping at her feet changed from black in the earlier shots to now a dark blue against wet white sand. Leave your face on, but once Melody has finished with Faith and Brenton she can change you for the day beach shoot position 4."

Picking up his camera, Cameron walked up toward the lighthouse to shoot position 2. Anton was already getting Fay and Robbie into the best position, the sun was still low, but cast an amazing hue, and the colour in the sky was beautiful. "OK guys, we don't have much time, so let's do this right the first time, OK?"

Katy had joined them. Her work was done for the moment: she'd handed Faith over to Melody to dress, it was too early to retouch any make up, but she always liked to be close by with each model's lipstick. She walked up to Cameron who was busy taking shots.

"Do we have another black wig?" Cameron asked.

"We certainly do, I'll grab it. I'll have to change her lipstick, but her makeup will be OK with the darker hair." Katy ran back to the tent.

Cameron continued to take photographs as Katy changed Fay's hair and lippy. The sun was pushing its way up and the wonderful yellowy orange tones were beginning to creep around the lighthouse and to bathe playfully around Fay and Robbie—the change in hair colour had worked perfectly.

"OK, work with me guys, time is against us; we need to get this done now. Anton, can you take that other camera and set it up for the next position? I want it low for the first shoot. Lucas, can you start lighting the tea lights? Be careful not to burn yourself or the lanterns. Is the canoe ready to go?" Cameron asked. A resounding yes was heard as the crew moved on to the next position.

A few minutes later Cameron wrapped that shoot. "Robbie, you're done for now, can you go back to the tent and hurry the next lot, I'll be ready for them in a few minutes. Have some breakfast and then you can get dressed for shoot position 5."

Moving around to position 3 all he could think of was the time, he had less than an hour and he wanted to get in all three shooting positions. Time would be of the essence, so he prayed he was doing the right thing in using Faith instead of Molly for this, the biggest shot of the day. He hoped like hell she wasn't lying when she said she took direction. Fay was OK to work with, and the camera loved her, even better with the darker hair.

Meanwhile, back at the tent, the atmosphere was growing tense. Molly had just finished looking over the revised call sheet.

"When did this change?" Molly screamed at Terry

"I have no idea what you're talking about. What change?"

"Here, it's been changed. I'm only in two shoots today, whereas they have four shoots each. What the hell is going on, how come they get more than me?" Molly should have been born with flame red hair; she could turn from cold to boiling in seconds.

"I didn't make the changes, and I didn't hire them, it's got nothing to do with me, you need to take it up with Cameron, he's made it abundantly clear that I am to keep my nose out of it," Terry yelled back.

"Well, you need to do something or I'm going to let loose. You're in charge of this shoot, aren't you? Then do something —or else! Molly warned.

"What shoot are you down for?" Terry wasn't interested, but he also knew he'd have to put up with her foul mood for the rest of the day, meaning that if he didn't do something to fix the problem there would be no hanky panky in the bedroom later.

"He wants me as a solo, in a black one piece, under the pier. I can't imagine that's going to be anything that'll make the magazine's cover. Look at what he's got them doing. What the hell, I feel he's fobbing me off, I've never been treated like this before!" Molly's flushed red cheeks should have warned Terry of impending doom, but being a typical male, he chose to ignore it.

"I'm going to have it out with him," Molly yelled as she stormed off.

"Just leave it the hell alone." Terry warned her, but there was no stopping her, she was on a mission.

Cameron was lying on the cool white sand, shooting Faith and Brenton as they slowly moved the small canoe forward through the water; the lit lanterns bobbing around them cast a sexy glow. "Can you both move forward for a kiss position, in 4, 3, 2, and 1, now! Perfect, love it, that's a wrap. Come over here and get out as carefully as you can, I don't want the gown wet."

It was then he noticed Molly standing behind him. "Hey Molly, what's up?" He could tell from the way she was breathing that she was angry. Chances were he knew why.

"What the hell do you think you're doing? I only have two shoots today? What gives them the right to have more? I work for the magazine. How dare you!" She hadn't realised that, as she was screaming at him, he was gently guiding her out of the way.

"Molly, it's like this. I love working with you, you do know that don't you? Well, today I have the opportunity of working with a set of twins. I've never had that opportunity before, so I worked the schedule to include them with Robbie and Brenton, mainly because of their suitability—they're all the same height, same build, same toning. I knew they would be dynamite on camera and they are, but I want you to shine all on your own. For you to be the centre of attention, where you aren't overshadowed by anyone, where you get to shine bright, as only you can."

"I am only thinking about you, giving you the best and most sexy shots. Trust me, when I've finished with you today, you'll be even more famous than you were yesterday. Are you OK with that?" He had to bite his lip, but he knew the stupid dumb blonde would eat up his ego stroking, and she did.

"I'm sorry, Cameron; I just thought you were fobbing me off."

"Oh darling, how could you possibly think that? You are my favourite model, that's why you're here. I made that happen. Work with me, babe, this is going to be a great few days. Now head on back to the tent and rest up, we'll be back soon for breakfast." With an air kiss and tiny pat on the bum, he sent her off with a smile on her face.

Cameron wondered how long he could keep her on a leash. Surely, she wasn't so stupid that she couldn't see what he was doing. It was Cameron's intention that Molly and Terry would grow to regret coming on this trip.

Ten hours into the flight from LA, he knew he was going to make them both pay for having disregarded and disobeyed company policy. Having Molly's boarding pass as proof was only the beginning. Cameron had a gut feeling that more was going on between them and, if he was right and they were an item, then they would be breaching another company policy. Time would tell.

"OK. Now come forward to the start of the pier. I want to catch the other side of the island as your backdrop. That looks fantastic, great. Now for some depth of field shots and we're just about done from this position. Yeah, that's it. Actually, Faith slightly lean your head back and drop just a little so that Brenton can look over you. That's it, that's an award-winning shot. Got it. That's a wrap for here. Now turn around I want to shoot you from the opposite direction." Cameron was on a roll, and he knew it.

As Cameron turned around, he noticed Molly was still watching. He hoped she hadn't heard his last comment. Last thing she needs to hear is that I've got an award-winning shot without her in it. Best keep my big mouth shut for the time being, he thought to himself.

The next shoot position went smoothly, the crew working together to make sure Cameron had everything he needed to do his job properly. Both Fay and Faith were brilliant; he had already decided that these next few days were going to be all about the twins. Molly and Terry didn't have a leg to stand on. Cameron had enough on them to cause them to lose their jobs if he decided to take it further.

"It's breakfast time, guys; you've done a wonderful job." Carrying his camera gear, Cameron walked back to the tent with Fay and Faith. The rest of the crew collected the props.

Thankfully, Terry had taken the hint to stay away. Cameron wasn't sure how long he could keep them at bay; Terry wasn't as stupid as Molly.

Molly was ready for the under pier shoot position 4, dressed in the black one piece. Faith and Brenton were ready by the small canoe. This time the canoe was on the sand dune in shoot position 5. Dressed in one of the blue and white outfits from Klassy Klozit, Fay was having her face changed by Katy, and Melody was dressing Robbie for shoot position 6 on the outside of the lighthouse.

"I need to make some phone calls; I need to get approval to do a few things. Give me a few minutes and I'll be ready to shoot Molly." He made sure Terry heard his last comment— he wanted to put the fear of god into him.

He called drug dealer Oliver, to arrange for him to bring an assortment of goodies to his room later that night. He had a taste for the twins and a renewed thirst for the pleasure of sins that Oliver could provide. Tonight he was going to party like he'd never done before. They didn't have to be on site until 3:00 p.m. the next day, so he was going to make the most of it.

Molly looked stunning in the figure-hugging black one piece; her ash blonde hair and smoky eyes looked the part as he laid her in a prominent position under the pier. With waves lapping at her feet, rays of sunlight streaming through the cracks in the floorboards above. There was just enough height above her head to balance the shot perfectly. Within ten minutes he was finished, much to Molly's disgust.

"What that's it? Just the one position, aren't you going to try different positions? She was fuming.

"No, Molly, there is no need. I have exactly what I want. You look stunning with the rays of sunlight beaming off your beautiful face." How long do I have to bullshit her for? The words echoed in his head.

Molly stormed back to the tent. Cameron wasn't stupid enough to follow her.

He asked Anton to bring the models to the next shoot position. The rest of the morning went according to plan. They wrapped the shoot at 10.45 a.m., packed up and headed back to the resort. Fay and Faith opted to go home when Cameron asked what their intention was for the rest of the day.

"I need a shower and sleep," Faith whispered in his ear.

"Will I see you later? I've arranged a delivery from Oliver for around eight this evening."

"How about we pick you up at 6:00 p.m., head out for dinner, then back to meet Oliver at eight?" Faith said.

"OK. I'll meet you in reception," Cameron agreed.

As Cameron walked to his room, he noticed Molly and Terry ahead of him. He slowed down and waited at the corner of the passageway to see where they went. He peeked around the corner to see them both enter the same room; he went forward to check the room number. He leaned in to listen through the door, but couldn't hear anything. I knew they were an item, he thought to himself as he walked further down the passageway to his room. It shouldn't be too hard to get physical proof, and that will be just another breach of company policy to hold against them.

CHAPTER TEN

Agree to Disagree

Molly and Terry enjoyed room service as they lay in the deep luxurious spa bath. Molly added some additional bubble bath, hoping it would release the tension from the morning's shoot.

Terry had avoided the subject; he didn't want to set Molly off on another tirade. He also wanted to make love to her before settling into bed for an afternoon siesta.

In all the years he'd worked with Cameron, he'd never seen him behave like this. He wasn't sure what was causing this change in behaviour. Was he threatened by Terry's position or was something else going on? He wasn't sure, but knew for the sake of the photo shoot he had to find out and fix the problem before it got out of hand.

The time delay back to Los Angeles meant there was nobody in the office to call at this time of the day, and he didn't feel like calling the head of marketing after hours—he wasn't that stupid. This was his first overseas project management assignment with the company and he didn't want them to think he couldn't do his job. He would see what happened the next day and if things weren't any better and he couldn't manage Cameron, then he'd have to make the call after the shoot finished late the next night.

Climbing out of the bath, Terry left Molly to relax and went into the lounge. Draped in the thick bathrobe, he sat at the dining table and went through the model portfolios that Ramon had given them the day before. He glanced at each of them: this time he focused on the twin's portfolio in comparison to Lucy's.

He had to admit the camera didn't lie; the twins looked just as good on camera as they did in print. But Lucy, she was stunningly beautiful, with her olive complexion, long dark brown hair and mesmerising big brown eyes. She stood out from the crowd and he couldn't understand why Cameron chose the twins over her.

All three models had their own striking features. Molly was a knock out, there was no denying that. Her body was perfectly proportioned with perky breasts. Her long ash blonde hair, black eyes and cheeky smile framed her face perfectly. But he was biased—he had been in a relationship with her for a few years now. They were in love and he didn't care about company policy. He knew for a fact that other employees were romantically involved so, if it came to the crunch, he wasn't afraid to name names. He didn't care who was caught in the crossfire; the company wouldn't fire everyone. He was well liked and respected and had been with the company for fifteen years. He felt confident they wouldn't fire him.

The twins had to go. For the sake of the photo shoot he had to fire them and hire Lucy. Molly would drive him insane if he didn't do something to make her the star. He'd promised her that, way before they even left LA, and had made it abundantly clear that it was he who pulled strings to get her on the shoot.

Pouring himself a whiskey from the bar fridge, he dialed Lucy's mobile; she answered immediately.

"Hello, Lucy speaking."

"Hello Lucy, this is Terry Henderson, the PR Manager from *This Could Be Your Life* magazine. Ramon gave us your portfolio; I know he called you yesterday to model for us. I'd like you to reconsider, I really want you on this shoot."

"Hello, Terry. I told Ramon that I wasn't interested. There are plenty of wonderfully talented models here on the island. I'm sure you will find exactly what you want. Ramon has worked with all of us, so he'll be able to find the right models for you."

"He has, Lucy, and that is you. Please reconsider. I can up the dollars, if that's the issue. Lucy, what can I do to change your mind?"

"No, the money isn't the problem; it's just that I've changed and this kind of thing simply isn't important to me anymore, that's all."

"Please model for us tomorrow night. It's a sunset shoot aboard the Mayor's yacht. If you don't like it after that, then that's OK. I won't pester you anymore. What do you say? Please, I'll make it worth your while."

"Well, what time would I have to be there?"

"Three p.m. sharp. Can you make it?"

"OK then. Yes, I can. I'm not working tomorrow." A smile crept over Lucy's face; she was actually looking forward to it.

"Is there any chance we can meet up so you can fill in the paperwork? And please bring your tax file number and bank account details." Terry was feeling rather pleased with himself.

"I don't finish work until eight tonight, but I can call past your room, if that's not too late for you?"

"Of course it's not too late. I'll have everything ready for you, it shouldn't take long." Terry didn't want to inconvenience her any more than was necessary to put her on the books.

With a smile from ear to ear, he was just about to go into the bathroom to share his wonderful news with Molly, when she walked out, asking who he was talking to.

"I have just convinced Lucy to model for us tomorrow night. So, my darling, you will continue to be the belle of the ball. Happy?"

"You bet! Yeah, no more twins; I knew you could fix it. Now let's get some sleep; I'm knackered." Molly was relieved and thankful. In fact, she was so thankful she showed Terry just how much she appreciated what he'd done as her tongue moved around his body, finally finding its rightful place as she teased the tip of his pulsating penis.

A few rooms down, Cameron was mentally and physically exhausted. Uploading the photos onto his laptop, he decided a bath was in order to relax enough to induce sleep. He allowed the lavender and patchouli bubble bath to do its job and relax every muscle. Fifteen minutes later he reluctantly dragged himself out of the bath and eventually fell asleep on top of the bed, not even having the energy to pull back the covers.

He woke a few hours later, showered, dressed and spent the rest of the time looking over the photos he'd taken earlier that day. He was impressed with his work. He loved sunrise shoots—the tones were truly magical. The way he found the perfect shot for each setting was breathtaking, but match that with the drop-dead gorgeous models and the results were pure genius. He was an amazing photographer, and these photos proved it. He uploaded them to drop box for head office to pick them up later.

At 6:00 p.m. his alarm reminded him to head down to the foyer to meet the twins. Oliver was going to drop off a party pack of goodies at eight. Cameron had already decided he was going to ask him to stay and join them. He owed Oliver that much.

Molly and Terry showered and dressed for dinner; they had decided to check out the local restaurants. They stopped off at reception to ask for the best place to eat along the promenade. Joan, the duty manager, was about to finish work. She recommended a quaint restaurant and offered to drive them. They accepted her invitation and chose a seat by the window in the foyer as they waited for her to finish work.

Molly was the first to sit down, her back to the window. She didn't notice Cameron jump into the back of the twin's car. Terry on the other hand, observed everything. He watched with great interest as Cameron walked hand in hand with one of the twins and witnessed a long lingering kiss between them as they jumped into the back seat. The other twin was driving. He continued to watch as they drove out of the resort grounds.

I knew it! Terry thought to himself. I knew something was going on between them. I should have thought it was something like this. The dirty bugger—and he's engaged. He's obviously having a good time here. It's good to get some dirt on him—makes my job easier when Lucy turns up and I get to fire the twins.

He chuckled to himself as he sat down. Molly looked up from the magazine she was flicking through.

"What's so funny?" she asked.

"No, nothing's funny. I just remembered what we did this afternoon. Would you like a repeat performance tonight?"

"Yes, please, I'd really like that." She wasn't lying; she enjoyed making love to him, pleasing him, making him whimper in excitement as her body teased him.

Joan joined them shortly after and drove them the long way to the restaurant. She was a true ambassador for the island. She would make an excellent tour guide, full of knowledge about the history of the island.

Joan showed them into the restaurant, seated them at the perfect table to enjoy the last of the sunset. Unbeknown to them, Joan had arranged everything with the owner, whom she knew personally. She asked his team to look after Terry and Molly and make their night one to remember.

That's exactly what they did. Terry and Molly were treated like royalty, waited on hand and foot. When they decided it was time to head back to the resort, Terry asked for a taxi. As they staggered out the door they couldn't believe their eyes, there was a limousine waiting for them.

"There must be some mistake, we ordered a taxi," Terry said to the driver.

"Sorry mate, all taxis are booked, there was only this left, I hope you don't mind. There's no extra charge," the limo driver told him. The hefty tip he got from Joan for the little white lie was increased by seeing the smile on their faces.

They drove back to Clairemont Resort on a real high. They tipped the limo driver, thanked him profusely and made their way into reception. Terry noticed Gabby, the resort manager, talking to reception staff.

Molly opted to go to the room as Terry waited for Gabby to finish talking.

He told Gabby how thankful he was for Joan and the restaurant she recommended, and finished by saying they'd even travelled back in a limo because all the taxis had been booked out.

Gabby smiled to herself; she knew that Joan had carefully orchestrated every detail for them, ensuring a magical experience Terry and Molly would remember long after they left the island. Joan wasn't the duty manager by accident. This was Joan to a tee—she was a natural at making the guests feel like they're the most important VIP's, and that's why Gabby and the rest of the staff loved her. It also helped that Joan had a wide sphere of influence all over the island. The locals loved her kind hearted spirit and they knew she did what she did out of love. They were always ready and willing to make any situation work out the way she planned for her guests. Goodwill breeds goodwill; everyone benefitted from it.

Gabby wondered if Joan had made arrangements to finish the night off for Terry and Molly, with a complimentary bottle of champagne and strawberries beside their bed. Of course she did, why am I even questioning it? Gabby thought as she headed off to her apartment to spend time with her husband, Michael.

Terry turned the corner of the passageway to his room and stopped short as he noticed Cameron fumbling with the key to his room. Both twins trying to help him, but none were capable of getting the key in the door. Disgusting, he thought to himself, he's smashed. I hope he hasn't brought a bad name on the company. He watched with interest the three of them; the girls were wearing next to nothing, short dresses, way too short. He couldn't tell for certain, but was almost convinced they weren't wearing any underwear.

He found himself straightening his shorts to try to stop his growing erection. This was ludicrous—he had no idea why this observation gave him a hard on.

As he entered his room, Molly asked what time Lucy was popping in.

"She'll be here at eight. It's OK; we have a few minutes before she arrives."

Terry put all the paperwork together for her to read and sign. It should only take a few minutes. He was looking forward to going to bed, his arousal was still there, he was going to enjoy making love to Molly tonight; whether or not it was her that filled his thoughts, the act would be worth it.

Lucy finished her cleaning duties at Clairemont Resort a few minutes early; she quickly changed and made her way to Terry's room. As she rounded the corner, she noticed a familiar figure further up the passageway. No, that can't be, she thought to herself. There is no way he would be here in the resort.

Even though he had his back to her, there was no mistaking him. His figure was etched in her brain; an image she wished she could wipe from her memory, but she knew only one thing would ever bring her that satisfaction.

She stopped outside Terry's door and knocked. All the time her eyes were focused squarely on Oliver. As Terry opened the door, she noticed Cameron and the twins escort Oliver into their room.

Terry, too, had seen what happened. He wondered who the lanky, longhaired guy was going into Cameron's room.

"Lucy, come on in. I'm Terry and this is Molly, the other model."

"Hello, nice to meet you." Lucy was seething, but tried to retain her composure.

Some fifteen minutes later, Lucy departed the room. She waited for Terry to close the door before walking up a few doors to where Oliver had entered the room. What was he doing here with Fay and Faith, she wondered?

She was friends with the twins; she wondered if she should tell them what Oliver, was capable of, but she was too scared to form the words.

She stood with her ear to the door trying to listen to what was happening inside. Music was all she could hear, no voices, just music. Was he still in there or had he already left when she was with Terry?

She had warned him many times never to step foot in her workplace, never was he to invade her personal space, or her working environment.

She left the sanctuary of the resort and sat in her car, shaking with fear. She waited for what seemed hours before she found the courage to drive home.

Oliver was thrilled to be invited to join Cameron. As a general rule he chose not to associate with his clients, but something about Cameron was different. He was a guest and only here for a short time, so it didn't matter what went down. He'd allow himself this once to just sit back and enjoy their company while they enjoyed his party pack.

Oliver knew the twins; he'd been supplying them with goodies for many years. He didn't know them personally; in fact, he didn't know anyone on the island personally. He had never allowed himself that luxury. It was imperative he keep his private life private.

He had felt a connection to Cameron ever since the day he met him on the ferry. Cameron offered Oliver a seat and a beer, and then settled himself back on the sofa between the twins. Oliver unpacked his party bag; Cameron looked down at the stash and went straight for the cocaine. The twins started more slowly—they wanted to enjoy the evening before getting wasted, well more wasted than they already were. The two bottles of wine over dinner had started them off nicely. Cameron invited Oliver to join them; he too went for the cocaine. Oliver was very strict on his usage; the last thing he wanted was to become a drug addict, well any more than he already was. It was one thing to supply drugs, but to use the product, well that just ate into his profit. Yes, he enjoyed a joint, but unless he desperately needed it, he didn't usually partake in the hard stuff.

Tonight, he had other things on his mind; he wanted a piece of the twins. They'd always intrigued him and, as this was the only opportunity he'd have, he was going to make the most of it. He finished snorting his coke, sat back down on the chair and listened as Cameron and the twins talked about the day's shoot. It didn't take them long to forget that Oliver was sitting in the corner of the room.

It was around 10:00 p.m. when Oliver dropped a roofie into their drinks. It became abundantly obvious they had totally forgotten he was in the room, especially as Cameron started making love to both of them while he sat watching. The live show was more than he could have hoped for; their inhibitions gone, they performed acts that men paid a fortune to see. The stirring in his loins grew strong and he knew he would only kick himself later if he didn't enjoy what was on offer here tonight.

As Cameron made love to one of the twins, the other twin started stimulating herself. Oliver watched with interest, knowing that very soon he would be stimulating her with his tongue. He'd tease her until she shuddered all over with excitement, then and only then would he slowly make love to her.

He took his eyes off her for only a second to notice that Cameron had passed out completely. The twin was head first in his groin, she didn't appear to be moving, but her mouth was still making sucking noises. He knew the roofie had worked. The twins were now his to do as he pleased.

Oliver moved in on the twin still trying to satisfy herself. He started by sucking her nipples as his hand made its way down her body; finding the right spot, his hand was replaced with his mouth, and he stayed there until he was ready to move inside her.

It wasn't long before she had mounted him fully. He groaned as he came quickly. The twin didn't seem to mind; in fact, she continued to pleasure him until his rock hard penis was ready for the next wave of excitement. This time he allowed himself the pleasure of exploring every part of her.

Once finished, he waited long enough for her to fall asleep. It was then he carried the other twin to the bedroom, where he locked the door and spent the next two hours doing everything imaginable. She was in her element, anticipating every move he made; the more she came, the more turned on he became. He was thankful she kept repeating Cameron's name, knowing that when she woke in the morning she would associate that sexual encounter as being with Cameron. He was in the clear.

At 4:00 a.m., he let himself out of the hotel room; he'd arranged their bodies to look as though they'd had a wild night, as they certainly did—just not in the way they'd intended.

CHAPTER ELEVEN

Surveillance

As Gabby walked past the real estate office, Susan waved her inside. She seemed sad, remote and solemn.

"Are you OK; you're not your bubbly self, what's up?" Gabby was interested to find out what was going on. Maybe she had found out what her daughter was up to.

"You're never going to believe what's just happened. Emily has just found out she's pregnant. I couldn't believe it. I thought she was saying it just to get attention, but Scotty confirmed it. Seems she got pregnant on her sixteenth birthday; some of the local lads got her drunk; gave her some drugs and took advantage of her. She won't tell me who they are, but I'll bloody kill them when I find out. What in the hell am I supposed to do with a pregnant teenager? You know as well as I do what it's like; the island is very small when it comes to its residents, too small to hide dirty little secrets like a sixteen-year-old pregnant schoolgirl with no boyfriend." Susan was livid.

"What about Dwayne, how did he take it?" Gabby was

curious, she knew the family unit had broken down.

"Not good, Gabby. Dwayne won't speak to Emily; he won't even look at her. He seems pissed off with me because I am supporting her and not siding with him. Honestly, I don't know what to do—seems I'm damned if I do and damned if I don't. He's so high and mighty; he's blaming me for everything. He's said he will disown her unless she tells him who the father is. You should have heard him. I thought he was going to kill her.

"I want her to have an abortion; no good can come from her having this child. I'm not in a position to help her bring a child into this world. I'm only just making ends meet as it is. A baby costs a lot of money and I only have enough to get by, business is not that good. No use asking Dwayne for any support, he's totally against it. What if she has the baby and turns out to be a pathetic mother? To be perfectly honest, I'm not sure I want to step into that role again. I just don't know what to do."

"I'm sure things will work out OK, just give it some time." Gabby tried desperately to reassure her.

The police officer in her was piecing everything together. When did Emily get pregnant? Yes, she is sixteen now, but when did she conceive, was it really on her birthday? Who drugged her? How did they get the drug? Who else knows about the rape? Who is the father? How old is the father? Could it be Oliver? What was their relationship all about? Why did she have an uneasy feeling in the pit of her stomach every time she thought of Oliver? She must get Katrina to see if he has a police record.

"Hey, what's up, it sounded urgent?" Katrina asked Gabby.

"Come sit. You aren't going to believe this." Gabby was still coming to terms with it herself.

"I was walking past the real estate earlier today when Susan called me in.

She told me that Emily has just found out she's pregnant. Apparently, she doesn't know who the father is. She told Susan that she got drunk, some kids gave her some drugs and took advantage of her."

"Interesting, if drugs are into the school scene, I definitely need to identify the source before something untoward happens. The last thing we need is a teenage death. It's time to ramp up surveillance, but who do we target first?" Katrina pondered.

"In our observation of Emily over the last week, she seems to spend all her time at Oliver's house and school, I reckon now with this revelation, we should follow him for a bit and see what he's up to. I'd love to know what's happening behind his front door."

They both nodded.

"OK, so how do you want to run this one?" Gabby asked.

"Let's go down to the pier, see if he's working today."

They grabbed a takeaway coffee and settled in a side street where they could watch passengers and crew disembark.

While they waited, they chatted about Emily. Katrina was trying to get a picture of the kind of person she was, but unfortunately Gabby didn't know her that well, just enough to say a casual hi to, that was about it.

"How was Susan, do you know if she wants to take this further? What about her husband, you said they're separated, right? Does he live here on the island? Does he know? What did he have to say about the pregnancy?"

"Wow . . . Slow down. Susan wants her to have an abortion, cos she doesn't want to bring up a kid if Emily proves to be a useless mum. Juggling a business and a kid isn't what she signed up for. Dwayne, yes, he lives on the island. He was livid; he's threatened to disown her if she doesn't reveal who the father is."

"Do you think Oliver could be the father of the baby, I

mean he's obviously got opportunity?" asked Gabby.

"I don't know. I suppose we can always do a DNA test, but they haven't reported it so we can't really stick our nose in yet. Although we could bring him in for questioning in relation to the drugs, but on paper he looks squeaky clean. We'll keep an eye on him for a couple of days and see if we can figure out what's going on. We may be able to shed some light on his relationship with Emily, but I don't want to tip anyone off about our drug surveillance, not yet," Katrina replied.

When Katrina had sourced the crew list, she put them through the police database, but nobody jumped out as a red flag, which annoyed her. She was secretly hoping someone had form, but unfortunately no one did. She was thankful Gabby had suggested using the resort car, which made the surveillance easier and less conspicuous.

Just as they finished their coffee they noticed Oliver make his way toward the ferry. "Looks like he's on the afternoon shift. Do you want to follow him to Sydney?" Katrina asked.

No, Michael would never allow me a free pass to waste all that time on a ferry to follow a suspect, he's already reminded me: "You aren't a cop anymore, you're a resort manager, Gabby. A few hours here and there are all I can allow for you to help Katrina, nothing more, do you understand?" Gabby mimicked with a wicked smirk on her face.

The two of them laughed it off, but there was something more going on and Katrina needed to find out. Gabby suggested Katrina jump on-board and carefully monitor the actions of the crew doing the afternoon shift to Sydney. It would be interesting to see if any of the crew stayed overnight and, if so, where they frequented, and whom they met up with.

"Who are you still connected with in Sydney; is there

someone who could do surveillance with you?" Gabby asked.

"Yes, I have a couple of guys that I still keep in contact with. I'll give them a call to see if they feel like doing some freelance work with me."

"Just promise you won't do anything stupid, and don't go out by yourself. I've lost count of how many times I've been on surveillance and witnessed another crime and been unable to do anything about it at the time. Just remember you aren't part of the Sydney police force anymore. If you see something, it's best you have someone else with you so they can follow it up," Gabby spoke from experience.

"Yeah, I know, and if they can't assist tonight, then I will just see what unfolds, trust my gut and use my best judgment," Katrina replied.

"OK, well you had better hurry up, looks like they are getting ready to sail." Gabby pushed her forward.

"Keep me posted, OK? Call me if you decide to stay in Sydney and especially if you crash at a motel for the night, and please be careful, OK!"

"OK, I hear you! I've gotta go." Katrina ran off with a spring in her step.

Just as well she decided to wear civilian clothes, Gabby thought, as she watched the ferry until it was well out to sea. She would have loved to be there with Katrina, but she knew Michael would never have allowed it.

On her way back to the resort, Gabby noticed Susan coming out of the bank. She parked the car and casually made her way in Susan's direction.

"Hi, Susan, how are things going?" Gabby asked.

"Not too good at all, Gabby. I can't for the life of me talk to Emily, not that she's ever at home. I suppose she's staying with her friend Hayley. Dwayne won't return my calls; the last he said was that he'd disown Emily if she didn't tell him who the father is. As far as I know, he hasn't called her, so I suppose he meant it. I just don't know what to do. I'm going to see Scotty next. I thought I'd better start looking at what alternatives we have, I have no idea who to call to get an abortion and whenever I mention it to Emily, she storms out of the house and I don't see her for days. I'm at my wits end with that girl."

Gabby wished she could give her some reassurance, but it sounded like Emily's secret hideout was still very much a mystery at the Olsen house.

"I'm sure it will all sort itself out. Emily will have to talk to you soon about her future; she doesn't have anyone else to talk to, does she?" Gabby enquired.

"I was just in the bank, but Jenny, Hayley's mum, wasn't working today. I'll call around to their house later; Emily has been spending most of her time there, so chances are she's mentioned it to Hayley or her mum. Maybe they have talked through the whole abortion scenario." Susan certainly hoped so.

"Well, let me know if there is anything I can do to help, even if it's just a shoulder to cry on, OK?" Gabby's hug lingered a moment longer than normal.

"Thanks, Gabby, I really appreciate your support," Susan replied as she climbed into her car.

As Gabby drove back to the resort she wondered what would unfold when Susan called in to see Jenny. Would Jenny reveal that Emily was not spending as much time there as Susan assumed? Gabby made a note in her diary to call past the real estate office the following day. She was curious to find out what Jenny would tell Susan.

Katrina settled into her seat aboard the Clairemont ferry; she was thankful to be located upstairs beside the window. She had a great view of the deck and could clearly see Oliver as he went about setting sail.

She wasn't too perturbed about the crew during this stage;

it was more a case of finding out what they did once out to sea and then after docking. She remembered the café opposite the ferry terminal, and hoped it would still be open when she arrived, as it might be her only chance to eat for quite some time.

Taking a seat outside with her back to the wall of the cabin, sheltering from the wind, she called Sean, one of her best friends. She'd joined the police force with Sean—they had hit it off instantly, becoming best buddies. It was during their initial training that Katrina suspected he was gay and, after confronting him, she became one of the few people to know his secret. Thankfully, his happy go lucky attitude and weird sense of humour allowed him to fit in with his peers in a work environment, but also allowed him the freedom to choose when to socialise with them. His privacy was crucially important to him, so he'd found ways of getting around the Friday night drinks, by immersing himself in additional study. Being a police officer was extremely rewarding and he loved his job, but he also knew it would not be his career forever, so he was preparing himself now for other career opportunities. There would come a time when his secret would come out and when that happened, he was going to be ready to pick up a new career elsewhere. There would be no transition period. He'd seen the bullying of other gay and disabled personnel in the police force and he wanted no part of that treatment, intentional or not.

Katrina knew he would be doing nothing except study tonight; his present position, implementing the training of dogs for the dog unit, was a nine to five desk job.

Sean answered after the third ring: "Hey, beautiful, what's up?"

"I'm heading over on the ferry, are you doing anything tonight?" Katrina asked.

"You know me, hon, just doing some study and reading, so

no, nothing that can't wait. Can I pick you up?" he asked.

"Absolutely, but can I meet you at the café opposite? You know, the one that does those amazing lamb burgers. I've been craving one ever since I jumped on board."

"Sure thing, do you want to stay with me, or are you already organised?" Sean enquired.

"I'm not sure yet, I'll explain everything when I see you, but if you get there before me, can you order me a lamb burger, and cappuccino, grab it as a takeaway."

"Order me the same if you arrive first. OK, see you soon," Sean replied as he hung up.

The sea breeze would change as they got further out to sea, but for now it was still pleasant enough to be outside. She rummaged through her handbag, grateful to find her note pad still in there. As she pulled it out, she started recording what she knew about Oliver.

Katrina was not at one with the ocean; she respected it enough to stay on the beach and admire it from afar. She knew nothing about vessels that sailed the ocean, but she did remember the name of the ferries that sailed Sydney to Clairemont Island—the Ro Ro passenger and cargo ship— only because of its weird name, it reminded her of Kangaroos. On her first voyage she was scared because she wondered if the crossing would be so rough the ferry would literally jump through the water, but of course this Netherland-built vessel did no such thing; its sturdy frame protected its passengers, crew and cargo implicitly.

She stood to move closer to the railing that overlooked the vehicles parked on the outside deck, they were mainly transport trucks that had delivered goods to the island. It was then she caught sight of him out of the corner of her eye; he was making his way toward the back of the ferry, behind the trucks. The Ro Ro passenger ship had space inside and out for up to three hundred vehicles. Katrina had transported her car over to the island on her first trip, but she was too preoccupied that day to remember what it was like downstairs. She was guided where to park and then escorted upstairs immediately. The same process happened when they disembarked: she was guided down to her car, where she waited for the tailgate to be lowered and then she was guided off the ferry.

She had travelled to and from Sydney on different days of the week and the ferry never seemed to be full or felt overcrowded, and that was no different today.

Katrina lost sight of Oliver; he was obscured from view. She carried on writing in her notepad, glancing occasionally down to where she last saw him. It was almost an hour later that she spotted him up on deck; she wondered how long he'd been up there for.

Settling back inside the main cabin, she casually observed the other staff. No one stood out as suspicious, so she allowed herself to drift off to sleep, waking with a jolt as the ferry docked.

She disembarked from the ferry and crossed the busy road to the best lamb burger joint in Sydney. Sean was waiting for her, he hugged her and air kissed her cheek, then handed her the coffee and burger.

Seated with views of the entrance to the ferry terminal, they watched for signs of the crew leaving. It hadn't occurred to Katrina that they might have vehicles of their own waiting at the ferry or that they could call a taxi or get someone to pick them up. She had presumed they would make their way on foot or via the bus which left from outside the terminal and in view of the café.

It was some thirty minutes later when she spotted Oliver make his way out of the terminal entrance and turn away from the café. She nudged Sean and they made their way along Smith Street: Oliver was on the opposite side of the street and about thirty metres in front of them. Both Katrina and Sean had followed many suspects over their time on the force. They knew the drill. In surveillance mode they separated, one on each side of the street, careful not to get too close, to keep the same pace and rhythm as Oliver, to blend into the background and remain unnoticed.

Oliver entered a café alongside a well-known strip joint. Sean followed him into the café as Katrina sat at a bus stop across the road. She trusted that Sean would blend into the environment and keep tabs on Oliver.

She took a moment to jot down the name and address of the café. Grabbing a photo of people entering was not an easy task as she had loads of traffic obscuring her view and most had entered before she realised that's what they intended to do. However, she got great shots of most people leaving the café. Not sure what Oliver's intention was inside—this left her guessing as she sat outside—she hoped Sean would fill in the blanks for her later.

Was he here to meet someone or just to enjoy an evening meal by himself? That was the million-dollar question. He didn't have any form (on paper), but that didn't for one minute mean he was squeaky clean, she wasn't that gullible.

She was genuinely intrigued by him, wondering what his story was. Why did he have such a hold on Emily? That was really weird; she couldn't wait to uncover what was really going on there, and hoped for Emily's sake it wasn't anything untoward—there was very little that shocked her these days.

She was interrupted by a message from Sean, it read.

He sat in a corner booth, ordered dinner. He was approached by a couple of the local ladies, who walked off in a huff, so he didn't seem to be interested in what they had to offer. Then about five minutes later a scrawny, pint-sized, heavily tattooed Asian man sat beside him in the booth. They had a heated discussion, which I couldn't hear, but an exchange was made under the cover of a newspaper.

The Asian man has just left, so try to grab a photo of him as he leaves the building.

As Katrina was busy reading the message, she just about missed the man leaving the café. She grabbed a couple of shots, but cursed because they were probably out of focus. The Asian man looked familiar; she wasn't sure if he was from her Sydney days, or if she'd seen him on the island. Hopefully the photo would bring something up on the police database. His car, a black Audi was too far away to see the number plate.

Oliver left the café about fifteen minutes later. Katrina couldn't wait for Sean to come out; she immediately fell into step with Oliver as he made his way back to the ferry. She quickly messaged Sean to let him know the direction in which she had followed Oliver, so that he could follow at his own pace.

The café opposite the ferry terminal was still open when she arrived back there. She waited inside for Sean to join her, and then they made their way to Sean's apartment where Katrina logged into the police database to upload the photos of the tattooed Asian man. Unfortunately, nothing came up; he was either clean or they didn't have him on their radar yet.

Over a few wines Katrina filled Sean in on everything that had been happening on the island and what drove her to being in Sydney that night.

Katrina and Sean may have been extremely careful in concealing themselves so that Oliver didn't notice they had followed him, but they did not notice that they too had been followed.

A middle-aged Maori man had also been waiting at the café. He was thankful he opened the door for Katrina and Sean to exit because, as he followed Oliver down Smith Street, he realised they were doing the same thing. He decided to slip further back and see what unfolded. There was no point in him getting mixed up in whatever was about to go down. He wasn't that stupid.

The next morning, Hōne noticed Katrina as she took her seat on board the Clairemont ferry; he was seated behind her. He hoped she wouldn't look around or remember him from last night, but just to play it safe he pulled the newspaper up over his face.

When they docked at Clairemont pier, Hōne waited until he could see Katrina disembark, then he left the ferry. He had a feeling she was undercover, but wasn't sure, so decided he should find out more about her. He followed her to the police station.

Whatever he was going to do, he needed to do it soon or risk missing the opportunity. The cops were obviously doing surveillance on Oliver, so Hōne would need to be extremely careful with his next move, whatever that may be.

CHAPTER TWELVE

Photo Shoot Day 2

The magazine crew stood in stunned silence gazing up at the private yacht owned by Clairemont Island Mayor, Denzel Woods. The well-equipped 122ft custom Burger tri-deck motor yacht oozed luxury with a capital L.

Ushered aboard and given a complimentary glass of champagne, Cameron found it hard to get into the zone and set up for the photo shoot. It was Lucy boarding the yacht that brought him back to reality.

Dragging Terry into the main deck salon, Cameron was furious. "Why is Lucy here, she said she wasn't interested?"

"I personally called her and it seems anyone can be bought. She is on this shoot whether you like it or not," Terry slammed his final words home.

As they argued they were unaware the twins had boarded the yacht and had made their way down to the opulent master stateroom where Katy and Melody were working on the models.

"I've told you, I'm in charge of the shoot; I hire the models, not you. You don't know jack shit about how a photo shoot works. I'm using the twins and that's final. Lucy can get the hell out of here; I'm not going to shoot her." Cameron was hitting boiling point.

"You're supposed to be a professional photographer—then take photos and leave the hiring and firing to me. It's my job, get used to it. That's the way it is and you can't do a bloody thing about it." The feeling in the pit of his stomach that was yelling *watch out* challenged Terry's determination to win the argument.

"Get out there and set up the shoot. Focus on the job, not your dick; yeah, I know you're screwing the twins. It's not going to work; they're not going to be part of this shoot anymore and that's final. Lucy has agreed to the rest of the shoot days, and it's just her, Molly and the boys, no one else. If you don't like my answer then take it up with head office in the morning, because that's exactly what I'm doing." Terry walked out of the salon.

Cameron was livid. He'd promised the twins they would be in almost every shot and that's exactly what he was going to deliver, to hell with Terry. Two can play at his game. He knew he had enough ammo on Terry and Molly to ring head office and dob them in. They could be instantly dismissed for what they'd done so far.

Screw you mate, Cameron thought as he went outside to the main aft deck where the boys were setting up the cameras. He wanted to capture all four models, the twins and the two boys, as they walked onto the yacht, and then take some more shots of them drinking champagne on deck, with the island in the distance, as they motored out to the private bay further around the island.

Robbie found Terry in the main deck galley as he steadied his nerves over a stiff drink.

"You may want to go down to the master stateroom;

there's a hell of a catfight going on down there—it's a wonder you can't hear it from here. Molly is out for blood—seems one of the twins told her the dress she was wearing was too tight for her fat arse. When I escaped the room, they were fair going for it, punching, kicking and pulling each other's hair out. Not sure, but I think Molly has ripped the gown from one of the local designers. Before you start defending her, yes Molly's arse was too big for the dress, but the twin could have said it nicer, just saying." Robbie couldn't lie if you paid him to, honest through and through, a quality that had served him well. Terry knew he was telling the truth, but how was he going to explain that to Molly, without her thinking he was taking the twins' side of the story.

Terry had left a message on Faith's mobile phone telling her they were no longer required for the photo shoot. How dare they blatantly disobey my instructions? The bloody twins, they're going to be the death of me. Terry thought as he went down to the stateroom wondering what the hell he was getting into.

Robbie was right: they were going for it. Mesmerised by the force behind each punch, Terry stood shocked at what was happening. He knew he should do something, but to be honest it gave him a hard on just watching them.

It was Brenton who broke the girls up. He'd eventually found the courage to get between them, overcoming his fear of being hit in the face. This was wrong; they were on the most impressive yacht he'd ever seen in his life. They weren't going to screw this gig up if he had anything to do with it.

Terry picked blood-soaked Molly up off the floor; he literally dragged her into one of the other staterooms and closed the door.

"What the hell do you think you're doing? How dare you risk the use of this yacht? What if you damaged something on it, do you know how much it will cost the company if we break anything? You're covered in blood. Oh my God, have you smeared blood on the stateroom floor?" Terry was shaking her shoulders.

"What! You think this is my fault, how dare you! It was that bloody twin, she insulted me, the bitch, who does she think she is? What's she doing here anyway, I thought you fired them?" Molly couldn't understand why Terry was telling her off and not the twins. It was clearly their fault.

He forcefully pushed her down onto the bed. "Stay here and clean yourself up; think about what you've done while I go and see what mess you've made."

Molly erupted into tears, why didn't Terry listen to her? He'd better make this right or he'd pay for it later, there was no question about that.

"Katy, how much damage is there, is there anything I need to worry about?" Terry asked.

"No, it's OK, I have it under control. Faith has a few scratches, but other than that she's OK. What about Molly, she was covered in blood, is she hurt?" Katy asked.

"I have no idea; I can't even look at her. Perhaps one of you can go in and find out how she is; I'm too angry right now." Terry was heading out the door for the bar when he suddenly stopped.

"Katy, who's ready to go?"

"Everyone, apart from Molly. I'll go in and see her now." Katy was putting the final touches on Faith's scratches.

"OK, get them out on deck and let's get this first shoot wrapped quickly." Terry was still shaking; he needed a drink before facing Cameron out on the deck.

Terry may have been stupid enough to think the yacht was soundproof, but it wasn't, and Cameron had heard everything. Brilliant, he thought to himself, I don't care how good Molly looks when she comes up, I'm going to tell her she can't be shot today. That'll piss her off nicely.

The photo shoot went surprisingly well. Lucy was indeed stunning in person and on camera, she worked well with the rest of the models, and Cameron got some award-winning shots. He was very pleased until he turned around and saw Molly dressed and ready for the next location.

"Oh my God Molly, what happened to you? You look terrible, did you fall?" Cameron asked.

"No, that bitch smashed me, that's what." Molly pointed to the twins.

Cameron walked closer to her: "Molly, sweetheart, look at your face. It's black and blue, even with the makeup I can see it plain as day, and that's a nasty cut on your lip and under your cheek as well. I'm sorry, Molly, but I can't shoot you tonight. I can see it and the camera will as well. You'll have to sit this one out; it's just as well Lucy is here, isn't it?" Cameron had to bite his lip to keep his composure.

With that Molly stormed back down to the stateroom. Cameron could hear her muffled sounds as she blubbered over the poor soul who had to listen to her. Aw, that's a shame, he chuckled to himself. One nil to me; ha ha.

He didn't see Molly or Terry for the rest of the night. The yacht moored at the pier in a private secluded cove that once belonged to Lenni Maxwell. Everyone went ashore for the last photo shoot of the night, set up as a high-end cocktail party and that's where the crew stayed after they wrapped the final shot. Champagne cocktails and nibbles—they were well and truly spoiled.

The trip back was pretty subdued; after nibbles and alcohol most of the magazine crew members were happy to catch up with some sleep, whereas Cameron had other plans. He crept downstairs to see what was happening with Molly and Terry; they had been absent all night.

He found them both down in the master stateroom where the girls had been dressing the models. The outfits had been packed up and were left in the main salon, ready for departure.

Terry had his back to the door and was working on his laptop; Molly was curled up on the sofa, sound asleep. He crept back towards the lower companionway to go back up to the rest of the crew, but saw Fay coming down the stairs. He pulled her into one of the staterooms, locked the door and made love to her as the yacht made its way back to Clairemont pier.

As the crew boarded the minivans to return to the resort, Cameron went to gently guide the twins into the van, but they declined, saying they were heading home for a good night's sleep. It was an 8:00 a.m. start in the morning.

Lucy offered to drive them home. On the way, she couldn't help but ask:

"When I was going into Terry's room last night, I happened to notice you a few doors down with Cameron. I also saw Oliver go into the room. What was he doing there?"

Faith looked at Lucy, dumbfounded. "What do you mean, what was he doing there? He was dropping off a party pack, that's what. Why?"

"I just wonder how much you know about him. Be careful, he's real bad news. I just wanted to warn you, that's all." Lucy spoke from experience.

"Yeah, he's cool, but thanks for the warning," Fay said as she closed the car door. She headed toward her bed; her body was aching all over. She hadn't had so much sex for ages, and it was starting to take its toll on her body, especially after last night. She felt as though she was battered black and blue. She remembered the tender but powerful way Cameron had made love to her, his best yet.

Cameron helped the boys unload the vans, and once the equipment, costumes and gear were safely locked away at the resort, he retreated to his room, absolutely exhausted. He was pleased the twins opted to go home, although he'd never have said no to some extra-curricular activity. At midnight he pulled up the covers and fell into a restless sleep.

CHAPTER THIRTEEN

You're Nabbed

Katrina slept most of the way back from Sydney. Once back at the police station, she checked her emails before deciding to catch up with Gabby at the resort. Gabby asked the obvious question, "So, what's the next move?"

"Sean said that, at the café last night, the Asian man and Oliver definitely exchanged something, but he was not able to grab a photo of it, so I think the next move is to search his house. I'll go back to the station, put an application in for a search warrant and organise with Sean to get a sniffer dog over for a few days to see what they can uncover. The exchange could have been anything, but if it was drugs, then I want backup.

"Good idea," Gabby agreed.

"I'll keep you posted," Katrina added as she went out the door.

By the time Katrina arrived back at the police station, Sean had already organised for Constable Aaron McKenzie and his dog Storm to arrive on the ferry that afternoon. They would be staying at the Clairemont Resort.

Within the hour, she had a warrant to search Oliver's home. She waited for Aaron to check into the resort and over coffee they worked out a plan of action.

With Aaron and Storm in place, Katrina knocked on Oliver's door. He answered almost immediately.

"Hello, are you Oliver Smith? My name is Detective Inspector Reid and this is Constable McKenzie with his dog, Storm. We have a warrant to search your property."

Oliver backed out of the way; Katrina walked past him into the open plan lounge and noticed Emily seated at the kitchen table, eating dinner.

"Sorry to interrupt dinner with your daughter, go ahead and finish it, this won't take long."

"I'm not his daughter," Emily said.

Oliver muttered under his breath: "It doesn't matter, Emily, they aren't interested in that."

"Sorry, what did you say?" Katrina asked.

"Nothing, I didn't say anything." Emily had seen the look on Oliver's face and was now too scared to say anything in case he got in trouble for her being there.

"Sorry, I thought you said you weren't his daughter." Looking Emily in the face, Katrina asked her: "You look young enough to be his daughter, are you a relative?"

"No, we aren't related, we're just friends, that's all, just friends."

"Is that right? How old are you and what's your name?" Katrina asked Emily.

"My name is Emily Olsen and I'm sixteen years old."

Aaron had walked around the lounge, kitchen and laundry area. Storm had only stopped briefly in front of the coffee table, revealing a half smoked joint. He then led Storm to the bedrooms. One room was clean but as Storm sat wagging his tail in front of a set of drawers in the room, Aaron asked

Oliver to join them.

Oliver motioned for Emily to go home; he didn't want her to see him get arrested.

But Katrina had other ideas. She wanted to bring their relationship out in the open, to let Emily's parents in on the secret rendezvous, and let them fight it out—while she focused on the drug problem on the island.

"Emily, just wait here, I may need to talk to you further," Katrina responded, making it quite clear that she was to stay put.

Aaron waited for Oliver to enter the room. Storm was now standing guard in front of the set of drawers.

"Open the drawers, please," Aaron directed.

Oliver started at the top drawers and slowly opened all three drawers. He then stepped back to allow Aaron to rummage through them. Aaron was unable to find anything incriminating in them, but Storm wouldn't move, so Aaron walked back to the drawers and pulled them out. Checking under and around the outside of the drawers didn't reveal anything either.

He then removed the painting of the Mona Lisa from the wall above the set of drawers, revealing a large safe.

"Open the safe please," Aaron demanded.

"I will have to go into the kitchen to get the key," Oliver said.

"OK, lead on." Katrina motioned him forward as she followed.

Oliver walked into the kitchen, opened the fridge door and rummaged around at the back of a Tupperware container. He grabbed the key and walked back into the bedroom.

Emily was now in the bedroom with them. Oliver opened the safe to reveal a large metal box and a petty cash tin.

Katrina moved forward and took photos of the boxes in the safe, and later took photos of the contents of the boxes on the kitchen table. She was no expert on illicit drugs, but the labels identified cannabis, heroin, cocaine, ecstasy, and numerous amphetamines. She was disappointed to see that, although there was a number of different drugs, there wasn't a large number of each drug. In fact, the contents could be construed as being only enough for personal use; she would need to check the guidelines.

The photos included shots of both Oliver and Emily standing beside the contents. She also took a photo of the ashtray on the coffee table with the half smoked joint. She did not ask who had smoked the joint; she didn't need to. Because Emily was a willing participant in Oliver's home and the joint was in full view, Emily had no option but to admit the existence of it.

Katrina escorted both Oliver and Emily to the police station, where she charged Oliver with possession of illicit drugs and use of cannabis. The weight of the haul was yet to be determined, but it didn't matter—he was caught red handed. The petty cash was far from petty, totaling a whopping seven thousand dollars.

As Aaron read Oliver his rights, fingerprinted him and took his statement, Katrina called Susan to come down and pick up Emily. She asked Susan to bring Dwayne with her.

Dwayne and Susan arrived within a few minutes of each other. Shocked by the phone call, they wondered what trouble Emily was in.

Nothing prepared them for what Katrina revealed about Emily's secret rendezvous at Oliver's home, or for the fact she was there when they searched his property and busted him for drug use and possession.

Katrina stated that, because Emily willingly stayed in the house, and because there was obviously some recreational drug use happening, Emily might in fact end up with charges against her, but they would worry about that later.

Katrina requested Troy come down to the station to advise Oliver of his legal rights. She called Gabby to let her know they'd caught him red handed, and with Emily, so that sordid affair would have to come out once and for all. In her opinion, it was a great day's work.

Troy hung up the phone, grabbed his keys and explained to Lucy that he was heading down to the police station—that Katrina had arrested some guy for drug possession.

"Did she say who it was; is it a local or a tourist?" Lucy asked.

"Yeah, a local. I think she said his name was Oliver."

"If it's Oliver Smith, you are not to represent him, I forbid it!" Lucy trembled as she spat the words out.

"What do you mean, you forbid it? What has it got to do with you?" Troy asked. He could tell from her reaction this person genuinely affected her, but he had no idea how or why.

"Tell you what, I'll go down to the station and find out what's going on, then, when I have all the facts, we'll talk about it, OK?" As he walked out the door, he didn't notice that the blood had drained from her face.

Lucy ran to the bedroom, threw open the wardrobe door, pulled down her suitcase from the top shelf. As it fell heavily onto the bed, she thundered down beside it. What was she going to do? How could she get Troy to see her side of the story? What would Troy do when he learned her dirty little secrets? She realised it was now or never. If she couldn't tell Troy now, she would have to hold her secrets deep in her heart till the day she died; there would be no other time when she could gently bring this subject up. It wasn't that kind of conversation.

Throwing random clothes into her suitcase, she had no idea what to pack. Where was she going to go? She would probably have to leave the island now; nobody would want to know her once this sordid mess hit the tabloids.

As she went to zip her underwear into the top compartment of her suitcase she noticed a small tin. She hadn't seen that tin in years, she knew what it was. She picked it up and threw it across the other side of the room. The contents spilled onto the floor: she walked over and looked down at the life she had tried so hard to walk away from.

Her teenage years saw her addiction rear its ugly head time and time again. She fought long and hard to conquer the highs and lows of drug life, and each time she thought she was free, someone or something would drag her back down again.

She gave way to the flood of tears that engulfed her; choking on sobs, she wondered how she was going to get out of this mess. She picked up the small bags of cocaine. These little bags of white powder had lain hidden in the recess of her mind for so many years now, she actually thought she was free of it forever, but here it was—once again she was being tested on her strength and courage, only this time she didn't know which one would win.

It was all Oliver's fault; every single time this presented itself he was in the background. He had ruined her life once too often. "No more. I'm not going to take this anymore. I'm not going to allow you to ruin my life anymore. I'm finished with you. You are officially dead to me," she screamed aloud. Words she had said many times before, but this time she actually meant it.

Lucy was still lying in a crumbled mess on the floor when Troy arrived home, tears streaming down her face, cocaine bags still clutched tightly in her hands.

"Babe, what's going on? Please tell me why you're so upset. Has Oliver done something to you?"

"I can't—I just can't. You will hate me," she sobbed.

Troy had seen the open suitcase and he wondered if this meant the end of their relationship. He was still patiently waiting for an answer to his proposal from three weeks ago. Maybe this was the answer. Maybe she was leaving him? But why and what does Oliver have to do with all this? He wasn't going to find out right now, she was in no fit state to speak, let alone have an intelligent conversation.

CHAPTER FOURTEEN

What's Really Happening?

The tension in the Olsen home was deafening. Emily sat at the end of the kitchen table, her eyes resting firmly on her feet. There was no escaping the fact she was in a power of trouble, and she knew she would have to come up with answers her parents would accept. Emily would have to come clean about her relationship with Oliver, and the discussion about drugs was going to be very interesting, especially if she revealed the real truth. Would they be able to handle the truth? She didn't know. Would the truth put Oliver into even more trouble? He was only arrested for possession of illicit drugs and use of cannabis; nobody had mentioned anything about trafficking yet, so maybe he wasn't in as much trouble as she first thought.

"Emily, I will ask you one more time, who is this Oliver person and how do you know him?" Susan demanded that Emily answer.

"I met Oliver about six months ago; I stay at his house most weekends. He's a really nice guy; he listens to me and doesn't treat me like a child."

"What do you mean you stay at his house most weekends? I thought you stayed at Hayley's place." Susan couldn't believe what she was hearing.

"Are you having sex with this boy? Is he the father to your baby? Is that why you wouldn't tell us anything about it?" Susan was livid. What else was she keeping from them?

"No, he is not the father to my baby. He has never touched me; he would never do that to me. You're wrong about him. If you only got to know him you'd see he's really nice," Emily pleaded.

"I have no intention of getting to know him. You are never to see him again, do you hear? Just look at the position he's put you in. If he were your friend, he would not have subjected you to drugs. Did you know he sold drugs? Do you take drugs, is that why you go to his house, to take drugs? Honestly, Emily, what has gotten into you?" Susan was on the verge of exploding.

Dwayne had managed to keep quiet and remain calm. He was waiting for an explosion, which would surely happen, around the time Susan learned that he had been aware of Emily's situation and had done nothing about it. Yeah, he reckoned that would be the straw that broke the camel's back. It would happen, it was just a matter of time, but he could wait.

Dwayne had suffered a heart attack the year before and, although he'd made great progress, the heaviness in his chest concerned him. Was it just stress or was he about to suffer another attack? He wished he had his medication with him, but that was the last thing on his mind when Susan called to say that Emily was down at the police station and needed to be picked up. Initially, Dwayne had told Susan to go and pick her up, what did she need him for? When he was told he needed to be there as well, he should have sensed something was up, but instead he grabbed his wallet and keys and raced out the door.

He rose from his chair at the kitchen table and opened the cupboard above the range hood. Fishing around in the makeshift medicine cabinet, he found what he was looking for, aspirin. He popped two from the packet and started chewing them. Normally Susan would check to make sure Dwayne was OK, but she was so worked up she was incapable of seeing logic.

"Emily, I asked you if Oliver is the baby's father. I want an honest answer, and I want it now; do you hear me?" Susan demanded.

"Mum, you are the one who doesn't want to listen. I have told you time and time again that Oliver is not the baby's father, we are just friends."

"Then who is?"

"For the millionth time, I don't know, OK!" Emily said, shaking her head repeatedly.

"Right. Then we are getting DNA taken to find out once and for all who the father is. Emily, because I want answers and we are going to get them now, not when the baby is born."

"Mum, I told you I was drugged, I have no idea who did this to me," Emily pleaded.

"Then it could have been Oliver, he could have drugged you. He certainly has had the opportunity, the means, possibly even the motive.

"Scotty has given me information on DNA testing and how to terminate a pregnancy," Susan said.

"What, you talked to the doctor about me behind my back, how dare you!" Emily was livid.

"Well, you weren't going to do it, and I'm certainly not in a position to bring up a baby and neither are you, you're still a child, Emily."

Susan decided the subject of drugs was more aligned with Dwayne; he'd been pretty quiet since leaving the police station so it was time for him to do his parental duty.

"Dwayne, ask Emily what her association with drugs is. I need a break, my head hurts," Susan pleaded.

"What am I supposed to ask, Susan? I don't know anything about drugs, other than the ones the doctor has me on for my heart attack."

With a heavy heart, Dwayne turned to Emily and asked his sixteen-year-old pregnant daughter if she took drugs.

"Dad, really!" Emily rose to leave the table.

"Sit down, Emily. Like your mother I want to know the truth. Now is the time to get this sorted once and for all. Let's be honest, you haven't treated me like your father for years, so it seems to me I have nothing to lose. So yes, answer the question, and answer it truthfully." Dwayne's tone told Emily he wasn't messing around.

"Yes, I did take drugs, not much but enough for me to forget about all the crap that's happening here. This last year has been hell for me. Oliver listens to me, he talks to me and he helps me with my homework. All the things you don't do. He treats me with respect, which is more than either of you have done in years." Trying to keep a level head, Emily pressed on. "He didn't want me to take drugs, I made him. None of this is his fault. He's never laid a finger on me, never."

"He's been charged with possession; did you know he sold drugs?" Dwayne asked.

"No, not really . . ." The surprised look on Dwayne's face allowed Emily to reconsider.

"Ok, I suppose I did. But I'd been going there for a long time before I knew for certain, and he didn't tell me, I guessed."

"Did anything change after you knew he was a drug

dealer?" Dwayne was curious. Oliver wasn't going to win any beauty contest, he was butt ugly and that scar was intimidating. What on earth did Emily see in him? Is he really this nice guy that she keeps saying he is? Has he never laid a finger on her? His gut was telling him a totally different story.

"Nothing changed, Dad, nothing changed after I knew. He's still the same person. Just because he sells drugs, that doesn't make him a bad person. You taught me to see the best in people, not to see their flaws, don't you remember that?"

"Yes, I did teach you that, but you have to admit he's old and pretty menacing looking; weren't you scared of him?"

Before Emily could answer, Susan butted in.

"What do you mean he's menacing? Dwayne, do you know him?" Susan demanded.

Here it comes, he thought to himself, heaven help us all!

"No, Susan, I don't know him. But I did meet him briefly, after we found out Emily was pregnant. I followed her to his house and confronted them. Emily swore there was nothing going on. I told her it was wrong for her to be spending so much time with a guy old enough to be her father, but she told me I had no right to interfere into her private life, that she was going to continue to see Oliver even after I told her she couldn't. Just like now, I feel that my role as a father has been revoked; it doesn't seem to matter what I think or say, nobody listens to me."

Dwayne stood to leave.

"Go on then, walk out, that's what you do best," Susan screamed at him.

"Just remember who started this whole thing, Susan. If you hadn't screwed around, we might still be a family, but no, you certainly put paid to that, didn't you? Any wonder Emily was drugged and raped, they probably thought she was an easy lay, especially since her mother is," he spat back.

"Enough, I can't stand this anymore, now you see why I

don't want to be around either of you," Emily broke into their argument.

"Fine, sort out your own problems, personally I don't give a shit," Dwayne said as he stormed out of the house.

Desperately in need of a drink, he drove to his local pub. He parked in a side street where there were no parking restrictions. He crossed the road and saw Oliver walk around the corner. No, that can't be right, he thought to himself.

Picking up the pace, he started to follow, catching him at the next crossing. "I thought you were arrested?" Dwayne asked Oliver.

"Not enough evidence and they only found enough for recreational use," Oliver smugly replied.

"You're friggin' kidding. Don't you dare have anything more to do with Emily. I know you've slept with my daughter, I just know it, and I'm going to prove it."

Dwayne dug his hands into his pants pockets, knowing he was so close to letting them meet their target.

"Good luck with that," Oliver confidently replied.

Feeling somewhat agitated, Dwayne knew he had to move away or make the situation worse.

"This isn't the last of it, you'll be hearing from my lawyer," Dwayne stated.

"Oh yeah, who's that then?"

"Troy Anderson, that's who," Dwayne said.

"Funny, cos he's my lawyer too. Seems that one of us is in a bit of a pickle," Oliver laughed.

Dwayne walked away before he punched his lights out. The sound of Oliver laughing made him even angrier.

Dwayne walked back to the pub, ordered a beer and thought about his next move. What was he going to do? He weighed up his options; he could beat the crap out of Oliver, which was laughable, he had never raised a hand to anyone. He could get someone else to do the dirty work for him, but who? He didn't know of anyone. He could give up and let Emily and Oliver be a happy family, what would that do to her future? Would Oliver look after her, help her raise a child that supposedly isn't his? Or would this be the biggest mistake of her life? Hell, he'd thought he was doing the right thing in marrying Susan, and look how that ended up.

Dwayne felt he was in a no win situation—he was furious, what was the point of a legal system if criminals like Oliver got off so easily? This just wasn't right, but what could he do about it? It was then he realised he needed to talk to Troy.

He knocked a little too hard, but he was past being nice—nice didn't get you justice. Troy answered the door. Startled by the way Dwayne stormed into his home; he was about to explain he should make an appointment to see him in the office the next day. Then realised he was here as a concerned father and knowing what they'd been through as a family, just this once he'd let it slide.

"Hey, sorry to barge in, but I didn't know what else to do," Dwayne said as he sat down at the kitchen table. "What the hell, Troy? I thought we were friends. How could you represent him, but more importantly how could you let him get off scot-free?" Dwayne demanded.

"He's not exactly in the clear, he will still need to go before a judge, but that won't be for months."

"There is more to it than that; you know it as well as I do. How are we ever going to find out what he's doing with Emily now?" Dwayne slumped further into the chair, as if giving up was his last option.

"I agree, but he wasn't going to divulge anything about their relationship and unless you can get Emily to do a DNA there is very little you are going to be able to do about it. Have you considered talking to her about getting an abortion?"

"Both Susan and I want her to have an abortion, but Emily

won't have a bar of it. I don't know how to make her see sense. I have a real bad feeling about this whole thing.

"Is there anything I can do to get the bastard?" Dwayne pleaded one last time.

"No, sorry, not unless something else comes up." Troy said.

Lucy couldn't contain herself any longer.

"Is this Oliver Smith you're talking about?" she asked.

"Yes, it is why? Why are you so interested in him? Troy asked.

"He's bad news, that's why!" she stated.

"He didn't have enough drugs in his possession to charge him with anything other than recreational use, Lucy, and he doesn't have a record, so I had no option," Troy answered her.

"Dwayne, I hate to tell you this, but I reckon he is the father to Emily's baby. He would have drugged her, he always does." Lucy couldn't help herself.

"Why would you say that, Lucy? You have no proof and Emily denies that he has ever touched her. What is it you know about him?" Dwayne asked.

She started to hyperventilate; she dropped to the floor, engulfed in tears and struggling to breathe. Troy and Dwayne tried to calm her; they could see she was really distressed.

"Lucy, you have to tell me. If you expect me to do anything I need to know the truth. Lucy, please tell me what he's done to you?" Troy pleaded with her.

"Nothing, he hasn't done anything to me, OK!"

"It's evident he's hurt you in some way, and if you tell me, maybe I can help you." Troy could tell Oliver had done something to her at some point to make her so angry.

After twenty minutes of hysterical crying, Lucy calmed down enough to realise she could no longer do this to herself, she had to come clean, and she had to get even with the bastard.

"He's a drug dealer; he has been for as long as I've known

him. He used to drug and rape me. It started when I was ten years old. At first I thought it was my fault, that I did something to make him do it. But as I grew up I realised he couldn't help himself; he needed to have sex and, because of how he looked, he thought nobody would be interested in him, so he would drug them first."

"Did you tell your parents about this, or the police?" Troy asked.

"Yes, I told my mother. She told me it was all in my head, that I was imagining it. Why would he do that to me? I was a child, why would a man want to touch me? As I grew older he stopped drugging me and told me it was my duty and I had to accept that I was his to do what he wanted to me.

Every time he did it he would tell me I was beautiful, I was his now and forever. It was terrible, nobody believed me; they all thought I was making it up," Lucy sobbed.

"Did you tell your father? What did he do?" Troy asked.

"Oliver Smith," she almost choked, "Oliver Smith ... . . he . . . he . . . he is my father."

Troy and Dwayne stood dumbfounded the wind knocked out of them. It took them a moment to register what she had said.

"Now I understand why you didn't want me to represent him, but Lucy, you need to tell Katrina This is the proof we need to arrest him, don't you see that?" Troy finally said.

"No, he will kill me—he will kill all of us," she pleaded with them.

Torn between wanting to teach Oliver a lesson and shelter Lucy from any more trauma, Troy embraced her, wiping the tears from her bloodshot eyes.

"You have to, Lucy; this is how we get him. If he did it to you, then yes, he is probably doing it to Emily as well, please help us." Dwayne pleaded with her, trying to get her to see reason.

"I can't, don't you understand, he will kill me. You don't know what he's capable of," Lucy sobbed.

"Troy, I don't care how you do it, but I'm coming back with Emily. Lucy must tell her what he's done; she won't listen to us, but she will listen to Lucy. Then we'll go to Katrina. He has to be put away for this. You know it's what has to be done, so hurry up and make her change her mind." With that, Dwayne slammed the front door and headed out into the night.

How was he going to get Emily to listen to Lucy? She was adamant Oliver was her best friend and he'd never touched her. He had to think of a way to get her around to Lucy without her realising what he was doing. He stopped at the Irish pub for another drink, hoping it would calm him down, but that didn't work. He was more agitated and confused than ever.

How could a father do that to his daughter? He couldn't comprehend how that was possible. How on earth had Emily let herself get into such a mess? Only Lucy would be able to get her to see the trouble she was in. Lucy had to tell Emily everything, then she would see sense, and then she would agree to have an abortion. He certainly hoped so.

He left the pub around 10:00 p.m. As he walked along the esplanade, he heard a couple having a massive argument; they were really going for it. He automatically started running over to help, but then stopped. "What the hell am I doing? I have enough to worry about without getting caught up in someone else's problems." Sitting down on the beach, he burst out crying; he had no idea what to do to help Emily. If only she would listen to him, if only he could prove that Oliver was not the innocent friend she thought he was.

CHAPTER FIFTEEN

Photo Shoot Day 3

Cameron woke early; he made himself a coffee and looked over the shots from the night before—brilliant, vibrant, breath-taking shots of the twins, Lucy, Robbie and Brenton. The way they looked together was just magical. He lingered over the close-ups of Lucy; my god she's stunning, a real knockout. He secretly gave thanks that Molly met with foul play and wasn't photographed; she would have only spoiled the balance of true beauty.

How was he going to keep her out of the rest of the shoot, with Terry breathing down his neck? Cameron was aware of how much Terry and Molly wanted the twins off the shoot. It had almost become a game now. Realistically, he would need to justify to head office why, from a professional point of view, he kept the twins in the shoot against Terry's advice. Damn it, the photos speak for themselves, I don't need to justify anything to anyone. I am the photographer, if the company doesn't respect my professional point of view then maybe I need to seriously consider going elsewhere, he mumbled to himself.

At 6:00 a.m. Cameron went down to load the van, double-checking all the equipment. It was intended that they wouldn't return to the resort until after the sunset shoot.

The Grandberry Estate shoot was booked from 8:00 a.m. to 8:00 p.m. with a break in the middle of the day. Catering was arranged to start onsite at seven and the shoot would start at eight, with horse and carriage shots, followed by couples enjoying high tea set up on quaint cast iron tables and chairs under expansive umbrellas on the manicured lawn, beside the man-made lake. They would then break for lunch and resume shooting in the vineyard at 2:00 p.m.

Terry had made it abundantly clear that the twins were not welcome on this shoot. He was met with a tirade of verbal abuse from Cameron. Cameron had then walked off in disgust and finished loading the van. He climbed inside and shut the door. Cameron did not make eye contact with Terry again until they all arrived at Grandberry Estate.

It was then he saw Molly. He walked up to her, fiercely shaking her from the shoulders.

"What the hell do you think you are doing here; there is no way I can shoot you. Take a good look in the mirror, you are covered in bruises, your lip is the size of a melon and I can see the scratch marks on your face—there is no way makeup can cover that. Katy is brilliant at what she does, but I'd lay a million dollar bet she can't fix this problem." He waved his hands over her face in an effort to demonstrate the extent of her injuries.

Molly, taken completely by surprise, stood dumbfounded, her lip trembled and eventually she let out an ear piercing scream of betrayal.

Cameron turned his back on her and yelled to Katy: "Katy, tell me honestly, what the hell can you do with that mess?"

Dragging Cameron away from Molly, Katy admitted that

makeup could cover the majority of the scratch marks on her face, and the bruising could be toned down, but she definitely would have trouble covering up the battered lip.

Cameron made a judgment call, but had no intention of dealing with Molly, so replied to Katy loud enough for Molly to hear.

"Katy, get the boys and Lucy ready to go for the first shoot position, they'll look great together with the Clydesdale. I want Lucy and Robbie standing side-by-side; together they sizzle on camera, so I want to take advantage of that.

Brenton and Robbie I'll do beside the horse and cart; the colours will balance perfectly. I'll call the twins and get them here immediately so they're ready for the second shoot position."

With that last statement he heard Molly gasp, taking in air as if taking her final breath. He refused to turn around, but could imagine the sight of Molly as she collapsed to the ground. Terry was the only one game enough to run to her aid.

The phone call to the twins was made. Terry was livid, but stayed out of Cameron's way. He agreed with Cameron, even though he'd never admit it. It was the fallout from Molly he was dreading. Terry had a few more tricks up his sleeve, but now, more than ever, he had to be certain when to attack. In the meantime he had to console Molly; the rest of his trip depended on fixing the situation in her favour.

The crew worked in unison. Lucy and the boys were dynamite. Katy started working on the twins as soon as they arrived and, ahead of schedule, the morning's work was complete. Cameron called a wrap and they broke to have their lunch.

Caught up in the moment, he had totally forgotten about Molly and Terry until he caught them out of the corner of his eye during the lunch break. They had kept to themselves, watching from a distance.

He could tell from her body language that Molly was ropeable. Terry was pacing back and forth which was a sure fire sign he was deeply troubled. Cameron slowly drank his coffee; aware Terry and Molly were glaring at him.

He knew he had not heard the end of this—there was no way Terry would let this go. From the way that Molly crumbled in a heap the night before and again this morning, he knew she would be out for blood.

Interrupted by Lucy, Cameron let Terry and Molly slip from his mind; he turned his attention to Lucy's questions about the afternoon shoot. Twenty minutes later he scanned the surrounds: neither Terry nor Molly could be seen. Cameron glanced over at Katy who had just begun working on Lucy.

"How's it going?" he asked.

"Yeah, great. Lucy won't take long, but can you send the twins over soon? I'll start them as the boys get dressed, we'll be ready for your 2:00 p.m. start," Katy stated confidently.

"Do you know where the twins are? I haven't seen them since we stopped for lunch," Cameron asked.

Lucy, Katy and Brenton shook their heads, indicating they hadn't seen them. Where were they? It was unusual for them to both be away from the crew.

Cameron walked around the buildings of Grandberry Estate, stopping occasionally to ask staff if they had seen the twins anywhere. Nobody had seen them, which just didn't make any sense.

"I saw them in the bathroom, but that was when we stopped for lunch. I can't say that I've seen them since, I'm not even sure they came back to the tent." Robbie commented.

Cameron tried once more to call them, but they were not answering their phones. He was at a loss as to what to do. It was so out of character; he knew they were happy with the shoot, so he could not accept they had simply left without telling him.

For a split second his gaze fell on Terry and Molly; had they done something to the twins? He wouldn't put it past them, but as far as he could tell they had stayed seated quietly in the shade of the stables all day.

"OK, we have no choice but to continue with the shoot. Katy, make sure Lucy and the boys are ready to go. I'll have to rethink how I'll shoot them, but time is running out if we want to wrap this in order to get ready for the sunset shot, so let's get moving guys," Cameron instructed.

Had he looked in the direction of Terry and Molly, he would have been shocked by their smirks of satisfaction.

The next two hours were a blur. Cameron tried desperately to concentrate on the shoot, but he was worried about the twins. What had happened to them and what was he obliged to do from a company perspective? He dreaded the conversation with Terry; he knew there was no avoiding the even more painful conversation with head office.

The twins went missing under his watch, after going against Terry. He wasn't sure how he was going to bounce back from this one. Maybe they would have no choice but to fire him. However, right at that moment, he didn't care about Terry or the company, his focus was on the twins and their safety.

He managed to get some half decent shots, but his heart just wasn't in it. He wasn't sure if the incident had affected Lucy and the boys, because the dynamic just didn't seem to work. He called an end to the shoot, even though he knew he hadn't acquired that one perfect shot. As he walked back to the tent he noticed Terry waiting for him, the smug smirk on his face was not the look Cameron wanted to see. He prepared himself for the inevitable backlash that was to come.

Lucy fell into step with him. "Can I call some of their friends and see if they have heard from them in the last few hours? If nobody has heard from them I can call Katrina for you, she's our local copper. She's really nice."

"Yes, that would be a great help, thanks for that."

He asked the crew to have one more look around the estate while Lucy made the phone calls.

"Seems you're in a bit of a quandary, how are you going to explain this one to head office? If you had listened to me and not hired them, none of this would have happened, would it?" said Terry. It's their fault Molly was beaten last night. This is all your doing, and I'm not cleaning it up for you."

Before Cameron could respond, Terry casually walked back to take his seat by the stables, leaving Cameron somewhat speechless. To be honest, he'd expected a tirade of abuse.

Lucy reluctantly revealed that none of the twins' family or friends had heard from them since early that morning. She had called Katrina and she was expected to arrive within minutes. The only thing Cameron had to do was call head office, but he would wait until after he'd spoken to Katrina.

Looking at the worried expression on everyone's faces, Cameron cancelled the shoot for the rest of the day. He knew they would be required to give statements to Katrina and he had no idea how long that would take—he sensed the magnificence of the sunset would go unnoticed that night.

Lucy walked to the front entrance of the Estate to wait for Katrina. She arrived at the same time as Dennis Faber, the owner of Grandberry Estate, returned from his day at the golf course.

Dennis jumped into recovery mode; he dispatched his staff to make another, more thorough, search of the property. Then he sat with Cameron, Terry and the crew as Katrina questioned them all.

The crew made their way back to the resort, unpacked the vans and, like a flash of lightning, everyone disappeared into thin air—nobody wanting to talk to or be with anyone else. The crew had totally fallen apart; it was evident there was no salvaging it. The photo shoot was finished; there would be no resurrecting it now. The only thing remaining was the phone call to head office to break the news. Cameron had loads of explaining to do; it would ultimately be the end of his career with them, that was a given. Terry would put his spin on things and, knowing his slimy reputation, the company would take his side of the story as gospel, and Cameron would have to defend himself.

Three hours later, there was a knock on Cameron's door. He hesitated, thinking it would be Terry again. He had honestly had enough. He never wanted to set eyes on Terry or Molly again.

He looked through the peephole to see it was the twins—they were hysterical, but safe. Scotty had medically cleared them and Katrina was satisfied with their account of what had happened to them.

"I was standing outside the toilet cubicle waiting for Faith when someone hit me on the back of the head. Then, when I came to, I found myself tied up, gagged and stuffed into the boot of a car. I could feel something beside me, something soft and squishy, but I didn't know what it was at first. Then Faith came to and I realised we were both together. It was comforting in that respect, but I had no idea who had grabbed us. Worse than that was the fear of what they wanted to do with us. My head was pounding and I kept blacking out all the time. I was scared, really scared," Fay said as she snuggled into the comfort of Cameron's arms.

"Did you escape or did someone find you?" Cameron asked.

"Faith and I eventually kicked the back seat of the car in

and once we got through to the front of the car we flicked the lever to open the boot and escaped. We were in someone's black Audi in the car park at Grandberry Estate. I'd lost my mobile, but Faith still had hers. That's when we saw all the calls from you and family and friends. It was then we realised you thought we had gone missing, and we needed to let Katrina know. She asked us to come into the police station and Scotty met us there. He checked us over and we told them everything we have just told you. We don't know who would have done this to us. We did think it was Terry or Molly, we believe they are devious enough, but don't think they'd have the guts to follow through. What do you think?

"At this point, I wouldn't put anything past them."

"I called Oliver and he's going to pop in after he gets back from Sydney tonight; I really need something to calm my nerves. I found some joints in my car; we can chill on that while we wait. But I'm starving, have you eaten yet?" Faith asked.

"No, I've been putting off a few things tonight, including calling head office. Terry was here earlier giving me an ultimatum. I'm so over the whole thing. I reckon we order room service, then I make the call, get it over with, then we can enjoy the night, what do you say?"

"Sounds like a plan," they chorused in unison.

CHAPTER SIXTEEN

Friend or Foe

At first, Hōne was unsure what he was going to do, having now located Oliver. He knew his loyalty lay with Tiny and the gang in New Zealand, but he was supposed to have done away with Oliver some thirty years earlier. So if he now revealed the whereabouts of Oliver to Tiny, then he would be signing his own death sentence. Tiny was all about honour, and trust, so Hōne struggled to see how Tiny would allow him back into the bosom of the family—the only family Hōne had known since he was a teenager.

The European gentleman who willingly followed Oliver, as prompted by Hōne, was quick to respond. Money was a powerful tool and Hōne was prepared to pay any amount to get as much intel on Oliver as he could. He had lots to think about, so the more he could find out about Oliver's lifestyle the easier it would be to take that next step, whatever that turned out to be.

Hōne settled himself into the café across the road from the ferry terminal; he waited patiently for Oliver to appear. This would be the third time he'd followed Oliver since first spotting him in the coffee shop weeks earlier.

Hōne had followed Katrina and Sean the night they had Oliver under surveillance.

Hōne had to be very careful; he had a rap sheet in New Zealand and was pretty certain it wouldn't take the police long to get anything they wanted on him. So he had to be extremely cautious in his movements, he didn't need to be inadvertently recognised or photographed.

On the ferry he'd asked one of the passengers the best place to stay. They suggested the Clairemont Resort, which was in walking distance to the ferry.

He had Oliver's address, thanks to the European gentleman, so he didn't need to wait or follow him home. He could quite confidently make his way to the resort and do further research tomorrow, after a good night's sleep. He walked in the direction of the resort and stopped dead in his tracks—the sight of the resort took his breath away. There was a massive cream brick building with what looked like two adjoining wings on one side and another massive building on the other side of the welcoming entrance. The oval driveway that led guests towards the entrance was bordered by lush green lawns and manicured gardens.

Hōne walked past chauffeurs waiting patiently beside their parked cars outside the entrance of the resort. He entered the pale blue and cream painted reception area which was furnished with contrasting cream and tan leather chairs with glass occasional tables. He could literally smell the opulence.

"Good evening, sir, how may I help you?" Joan, the duty manager, welcomed Hōne to the resort.

"Sorry, I don't have a reservation. This is sort of a spur of the moment trip. I was just made redundant and was drowning my sorrows in a pub in Sydney when I overheard a couple go on and on about their trip here. It sounded so great

I decided to jump on the ferry right away, before I talked myself out of it. So, here I am. I didn't even go home to pack a bag."

"How long would you like to stay with us?" Joan asked.

"To be honest, I don't know. How about the weekend, and then I'll take it day by day, is that OK?" Hone asked.

"Yes, that's fine. We aren't booked out, so you have the flexibility to take each day as it comes. Here is a map of the island and you will find plenty of brochures in your room with all the things that make Clairemont Island beautiful and unique. It really is unlike anywhere else in the world. Since you didn't pack a bag, I'll get housekeeping to pop a few extra things in your room, which should tide you over until you can get out and explore the island. The boutique here in the resort has everything you should need, but there are lots more shops around the island."

Joan allocated him a room in the west wing and summoned Jeff, the doorman, to escort him to his room. Jeff took Hōne the long way around, showing him the restaurant and bar and how to get to the swimming pool and gym. The estate had two swimming pools; one indoor beside the spa and the other was outside in a comfortable setting of tables and lounge chairs under giant umbrellas. Manicured garden beds and lush green lawns spread out as far as the eye could see. Hōne was suitably impressed.

They passed a very inviting bar, with soft music playing in the background and only a few people enjoying a quiet drink. The Zanzabar was tastefully decorated with rich mahogany leather chairs. Hōne thanked Jeff for the tour, but decided to settle into the bar and find the way to his room later.

Bar manager, Andrew Graham, had learned to steer away from personal chitchat, realising most guests wanted to escape their dreary or boring lives and preferred to hear all about what's possible on the island. This suited Hōne perfectly; he most definitely didn't want to get into any backstory, other than the lie he had already told Joan when he registered under the false name from the passport he had used to travel to Sydney. Nobody needed to know he had a criminal record; what good would it do them?

At 11:00 p.m. the rugby game Hōne had been watching in the bar finished; he was ready for bed. "Thanks mate, see you tomorrow."

Andrew gave Hōne the thumbs up.

As Hōne turned the corner of the west wing he spotted a figure knocking at one of the rooms. He reckoned it was Oliver—the lighting wasn't the best and he'd had a few too many beers so he wasn't exactly sure. What would Oliver be doing here in the resort?

He slowly walked closer to the person knocking on the door. Just as he got close enough to identify the person was definitely Oliver, the door opened and he disappeared inside. Hōne walked up to the door, stood outside it, pressed his ear against it to listen, but couldn't hear anything inside. What was he going to do, knowing that Oliver was inside this room? He was so close, and yet so far away. He hadn't devised a plan; he still wasn't sure what he was going to do. Was he going to confront Oliver, talk to him, catch up on the last thirty years, or would Oliver react immediately, knowing his number was up? Would Hōne be forced into making a decision he didn't want to? He had no idea. But, right at this moment, he knew exactly where Oliver was.

Hōne checked the number of his room key, looked at the door in front of him and went to the door on the left, unlocked it and walked inside his hotel room.

What was Oliver doing in the resort? Curiosity was playing havoc with him, so he quietly opened the door to his balcony, wondering if he could see or hear anything from next door. He could see the curtains next door were blowing freely from the evening breeze, indicating the balcony door was open. The familiar smell of marijuana wafted from inside. This resort was a smoke free zone, but people commonly believed that, as long as they opened a window or door, they could continue to smoke in their rooms.

Hōne could hear hushed voices. He climbed over the balcony barrier separating the two rooms, stood with his back to the wall, and listened to determine how many people were inside.

CHAPTER SEVENTEEN

Behind Closed Doors

Gabby Saintclaire, manager of Clairemont Resort, woke with a terrible feeling in the pit of her stomach. She acknowledged her gut instincts, always had, always would. Her gut feelings had saved her life on many occasions during her twelve years in the police force. Now that she'd retired, she still took them extremely seriously. On days like this, she trod very cautiously and warned everyone around her to be careful as well.

Ella Bellows was going about her normal duties as cleaner at Clairemont Resort. She knocked on the door of room 261: *housekeeping*, knock, knock, *housekeeping*. Not hearing any movement, she waited a moment before entering the room. Putting her headphones back onto her head, she settled into Adele belting out the words to *Hello*, as she pushed her trolley into the room and diligently started cleaning the kitchen area. She began by washing and drying the dishes on the bench and in the sink. As she went to wipe the tables in the lounge area adjoining the kitchen she noticed the glass coffee table had been smashed, shattered glass covered the floor and nearby sofa. Allowing her peripheral vision to scan the rest of the room, the overturned chairs, and random objects strewn everywhere was evidence enough for her to realise something untoward had happened in this room.

The bedroom door was open, she cautiously moved forward. The ghastly sight that lay before her took her breath away. Blood covered the crisp, white sheets on what had once resembled a bed. The curtain had been ripped off its tracks and lay across the open balcony door. The curtain was also riddled with blood. Ella could tell that someone had held the curtain as a defense mechanism—or maybe it had covered their escape route.

She turned slowly to follow the trail of blood that led to the bathroom. Scared to venture any further, but knowing that, if someone was lying in the bathroom needing her help, she had better act fast. With sheer trepidation, she started walking around the end of the bed. For a split second she wondered if she was putting herself in danger, and as a second thought, she pulled the bedside lamp from the wall socket. Armed with that as a weapon she cautiously walked into the bathroom, heart pounding so loudly she could barely hear herself think.

As she flicked the light switch on she was met with the most horrific sight imaginable. Instinctively, she let out a horrendous scream.

Gabby was in front reception talking to Joan, the duty manager, when they heard the scream. Scanning the guests immediately around them, their faces confirmed what she had heard. Reaching for the phone she dialed the resort's security room. "James, Reception NOW!"

Within seconds, James, the head of security, came running into front reception: "What is it?"

"I'm not sure, James. I heard the most horrendous scream,

159

and it came from the west wing. Can you please check. It may be nothing, but it certainly sounded like it needs investigating."

James cautiously made his way along the west wing corridor; he could see some guests nervously standing outside their rooms. When they spotted James, they motioned him to come closer.

"It came from that room," a young Canadian tourist stated. "I was walking past the room when I heard the scream, it was definitely this room." He pointed to room 261.

James asked everyone to move out of the way and phoned security for back up. Adam arrived within minutes; it was then that James knocked on the door.

The guest had been adamant the scream had come from this room, so James knocked on the door once again.

"Security, is everything OK?" He leaned closer to the door to see if he could hear anything from the room, but it was deathly quiet.

Standing with his back to the wall beside the door jamb, James unlocked the door. "Security, I'm coming in!" He didn't open it immediately, but waited a few seconds, just in case there was retaliation. When he felt the situation was safe enough to enter the room, he opened the door fully and, with gun poised ready for action, he scanned the room.

The first thing he noticed was the cleaning trolley parked in the lounge beside the kitchen table. Identifying the room was clear of danger, he was drawn to the muffled sound of crying. It was coming from the bedroom, and the door was open.

He cautiously moved closer to the bedroom; only to be met with the sight of the blood-soaked bed. He then realised the crying was coming from the other side of the bed. He slowly turned his head to follow the trail of blood and it was then he saw Ella slouched over and squatting on her knees at the entry to the bathroom; a smashed bedside lamp lay on the floor beside her.

His first instinct was that she'd been injured, but how and by whom? He needed to get a closer look inside the bathroom. He cautiously moved with his back firmly pressed against the wall. He didn't want to startle Ella. He was certain she was not aware of his presence—he hoped and prayed whoever was in the bathroom had not heard him enter. Apart from Ella's constant crying, he could not hear anything else, but that didn't for one moment mean there wasn't any danger lurking within. His fifteen years of training well and truly prepared him for this moment.

Slowly, very slowly, he crept towards the bathroom door. He was close enough to Ella to observe that she had no visible signs of harm. She must be in shock, he thought to himself. As he looked up he realised the mirror on the bedroom wall was directly in front of the bathroom door, he could see himself as plain as day. The trouble with that was whoever was in the bathroom could probably see him as well.

He had to act quickly. "Security, I'm coming in!" As he said it, he quickly moved himself into the bathroom and scanned the room.

He automatically turned back and fell to his knees in front of Ella. He looked directly in her eyes and asked if she was hurt. He knew from her face she was in shock, she didn't see or hear him. He scooped her up off the floor and carried her into the lounge and laid her down on the sofa. He asked Adam to call an ambulance. Then he closed the bedroom door.

CHAPTER EIGHTEEN

Under the Darkness of Night

Gabby called Katrina who made it to the resort in record time. Ramon was taking photos of the room. Aaron and Storm had followed the indented marks on the grass outside the room. Katrina and Aaron had surmised that the missing bedspread was used to transport a heavy object, possibly a body, across the grounds toward the car park. There was a large area of blood pooled on the edge of the grounds, but nothing spectacular. Storm picked up the scent of someone and a few minutes later Aaron called Katrina to inform her the scent led him to the ferry. He would check the security cameras and let her know the outcome.

The room was registered under the name of Terry Henderson. The magazine *This Could Be Your Life* was picking up the tab. There was no sign of Terry anywhere. Joan had called some of the magazine crew to see if any of them knew of his whereabouts. Katy suggested they try Molly's room as she suspected they were an item, and she said as much to Gabby.

It was then that Joan returned with Terry and Molly in tow. It appeared that the room in question, room 261, was at first booked out to Terry, but since he and Cameron were supposed to share a room, he gave the room to Cameron and instead shared Molly's room. Head office did not need to be advised who was sharing with whom, just as long as no additional rooms were booked to the company.

Joan settled the crew into one of the office spaces, away from the prying eyes of other guests. They didn't need to know what was happening in the resort. A few guests in the west wing were aware that something had happened in room 261, but nobody knew a crime had been committed. There was no physical body at the scene, just an overwhelming amount of blood.

James, the security manager, handed Katrina a report on the camera surveillance in and around the resort from the previous night. He identified that Cameron had entered his room at 5:30 p.m. Then, at 8:00 p.m. Terry Henderson knocked on Cameron's door and was allowed access. Terry left seven minutes later. The next to arrive, at 9:30 p.m., were Fay and Faith Ash. Room service delivered meals at 9:50 p.m. At 11:05 p.m. a hooded figure in dark clothing knocked at the door, and gained access. He was followed by another man who stopped at the door, but did not enter. That person entered the room to the left of Mr. Collins' room. That room was booked to a Mr. Parkes.

"James, when you did preliminary questioning of the guests in the West Wing, was Mr. Parkes questioned?" Katrina asked.

"No, he didn't answer the door, but I will go back now." James returned to Mr. Parkes' room.

He knocked repeatedly on the door of room 259. It took quite a few minutes before it was answered. James was just about to unlock the door and let himself in, when a sleepy

Mr. Parkes yanked the door open.

"Take it easy mate! What's going on—is there a fire or something?"

"Sorry, Mr. Parkes. I'm James Jollyman, security manager here at the resort. I'm sorry to bother you, but wanted to ask you a couple of questions."

"Please come on in. I've had a hell of a night, not sure I can be of much help. You've just woken me up. What can I help you with?"

"I'm wondering if you happened to hear anything unusual last night," James asked.

"Unusual in what sense? I think I must have eaten something really bad, I spent most of the night on the toilet."

"Did you hear any arguing, fighting or screaming coming from next door?"

"Yeah, around midnight there was a hell of a racket, but then I turned on the TV to drown out the noise and realised we both must be watching the same TV program because it sounded the same. After a while I didn't even hear their TV because, as I said, I spent most my time in the bathroom.

"In fact I need to head back there now, sorry to rush you but I do have to go."

"That's OK. I'm sorry to have bothered you. Hope you feel better soon. Can I send a doctor?" James asked.

"No. Thanks for the offer, I'm hoping this is the last of it."

As Katrina waited for updates from Aaron and James, Scotty said that nobody had presented to the medical centre overnight. There was way too much blood in the bedroom and bathroom; whoever was injured would need medical attention, unless there were multiple people injured.

Where was Cameron Collins? Where were the twins? Who was the hooded man? The security camera did not give a clear image—medium build, about 186 cm, dressed in jeans, a sweatshirt with a hood. He had a small backpack hung over the left shoulder. They must have all departed from the balcony door, which was not covered by camera surveillance.

Was someone out to do harm to the twins? After all, they had been abducted the day before. Was someone out to do harm to Cameron and, if so, why?

"Katrina, there have been two ferries leave since midnight. I'm waiting for a copy of their security camera records which I'll bring back to the resort soon, but they didn't notice anyone get onboard that was injured," Aaron reported back.

"Thanks Aaron. I found a trail of blood heading in the other direction. I'll follow that and keep you posted.

"Gabby, do you want to join me?" Katrina asked.

"Absolutely, just let me tell Michael."

As they followed the haphazard trail, Gabby asked: "OK, so what have we got, apart from missing bodies and too many questions?"

Katrina replied: "I think something is going on with the twins. I mean, what really happened to them yesterday? How come the person who knocked them out didn't take them off the property straight away? It was as if they were dumped in the boot of the car and then just forgotten about. Or were they waiting for the cover of darkness to get the car off the estate without arousing suspicion? Whose car was it, anyway? The twins said it was a black Audi, but they didn't think to look at the license plate, and when I went out to the estate to check, I couldn't find an Audi anywhere. It's not that I don't trust what the twins said; it's just that something doesn't feel right."

She called Aaron, "While you're at the ferry can you please find out everything you can about black Audi's, how many have been transported back and forth over the last week?"

"Gabby, you trust your gut instincts, what are you feeling about this case?" Katrina asked.

"It is on high alert. I woke up this morning sensing

something was up. In saying that, there must be a logical reason for what happened with the twins yesterday and what's gone down in Cameron's room. I agree that thing with the twins was left field. Who would want to harm them, they're just kids? Who could they have pissed off to put them in so much trouble?"

"Do you think it's drug related?" Katrina asked. "Maybe there is something else going on here that we haven't even considered yet. We know that Oliver has just been busted for drug use and possession. What if he works for a syndicate and this is payback? Maybe the twins are into this drug racket as well. It just seems too convenient that only yesterday we pull Oliver in, he's released with a warning, and the twins go missing, and now we have a bedroom full of blood."

Without quite realising where the blood trail was taking them, they looked up to see it was leading around the back of Oliver's house. They knocked repeatedly without answer. Then they noticed Emily lying on a blanket on the back lawn. Making their way closer, they could see her eyes were closed. Not sure if she was asleep, Katrina gently nudged her feet. A startled Emily roused. They knew instantly she had taken something. Her glazed expression was a dead giveaway.

"Emily, why are you sitting out here all by yourself?" Katrina asked. "Where is Oliver?"

There was no response.

"Are you OK?" Gabby asked.

Emily took ages to answer, it was if she was internally trying to understand if she was or not. "I am, but not sure they are."

"What do you mean *they?* Who is in there, Emily?" Katrina enquired.

"Them, those sluts, that's who!" she sobbed.

Gabby and Katrina slowly moved toward the back door. "Police, coming in" Katrina called out before opening the door and walking inside.

The trail of dried blood stretching across the kitchen floor drew their attention to the sounds of whimpering coming from the lounge room. Katrina once again announced her intention to enter the room: "Police, I'm coming in."

There was no movement whatsoever. The twins were sitting on the coffee table, crying, their eyes fixed firmly on Cameron who was lying on the sofa, smothered in blood. Katrina lifted the once-white towel from his body to reveal a deep stab wound that looked to be in his upper arm: he was unconscious. Katrina felt for a pulse; it was faint and thready, but he was alive. "He needs to get to the medical centre," Katrina said urgently. Gabby quickly called for an ambulance.

"No, we have to stay here and wait for Oliver. He told us to wait for him, we can't go anywhere," Faith pleaded.

"What do you mean, Oliver told you to wait here? Where is he?"

"We don't know. He told us to run to his house and wait for him."

"How did Cameron get stabbed?" Gabby asked Faith.

"I'm not sure; it's all a bit of a blur. We were in Cameron's room when all of a sudden Oliver noticed someone outside. He told us to get the hell out, to save ourselves, and to meet back at his place.

"Cameron pushed us into the bedroom, locked the door and we thought we were safe. It was then Fay saw that Cameron was bleeding really bad. We put him on the bed and grabbed towels from the bathroom to stop the bleeding. The fighting was getting really loud and we got scared. Then Fay suggested we move him into the bathtub to keep the mess from the blood contained., So we dragged him into the bathtub, grabbed more towels and we wrapped them around his shoulder and held on tight to stop the bleeding, and it did, but took ages. Eventually the noise stopped and when we came out of the bathroom, the room was empty. Nobody was there, nobody. Curtains were pulled off their tracks in the bedroom, and the bed was covered in blood. I know we put Cameron onto the bed, I suppose we made all that mess. I'm sorry about that, I didn't think. The lounge was a mess, furniture tipped over, the coffee table smashed, I think there were even holes in the wall.

"Oliver had told us to meet him back at his house, so we came here, but he hasn't turned up."

"Did you see the other person? Do you know who it was?" Katrina asked.

"No, I've no idea who it was. I don't think any of us got a look at him, we were so busy trying to get to the bedroom."

"Do you know what's happened to Emily out there? If I'm not mistaken, I believe she is stoned out of her mind."

"She was here when we arrived. At first she wasn't going to let us in. When we said Oliver told us to meet him here, she opened the door, but she lost it when she saw all the blood. It took ages to get the bleeding under control again."

"She must have overheard us talking about what had happened. I think I said that someone is bound to be dead, looking at the state of the room. Then she disappeared. I thought she must have gone home. I didn't realise she's been outside all this time," Faith said.

Once everyone was in the ambulance, Gabby and Katrina walked back to the resort. James and Aaron were waiting for them. Katrina explained what the twins had said.

"Yes, I can see that scenario is plausible—they all agreed. But where is Oliver? Did he escape and, if so, what condition is he in?"

"I had a phone call from Katy, one of the magazine crew. She wanted to let me know that Terry and Cameron had been at each other's throats for days. Seems the twins have been getting preferential treatment on the shoot and the model

Molly was not too happy about that. Terry and Molly have confirmed to me that they are an item, so I think we could pull them back in for questioning. They definitely have means, motive and opportunity to attack the twins, and also to take matters further with Cameron. Maybe it was a hit on Cameron, and Oliver got caught in the crossfire. Maybe the two of them put the twins out of action yesterday, hoping to get them out of the way once and for all."

"That certainly sounds possible, let's pull them in."

CHAPTER NINETEEN

Please Believe Me

Dwayne drifted in and out of sleep; for hours he would stare at the bare walls, wondering what he was going to do now. The bottle of Bourbon that sat beside his bed slowly emptied. The contents gave him no relief whatsoever.

As morning approached, Dwayne ate his breakfast, had his tablets and then put the container into his pocket; if today was going to be as confrontational as he assumed it would be, he suspected he might need to have them on hand.

With a heavy heart he knocked at the front door and waited for a reply. Susan answered.

Taken aback by Dwayne's presence, she asked what he wanted.

"We need to talk to Emily, is she up yet?"

Susan started crying: "I don't know where she is. She's probably with him."

"We're going around there. There's been some progress, and this needs to get sorted today. We can't wait any longer."

Susan grabbed her bag and jumped into the passenger seat

as Dwayne drove the few blocks to Oliver's home. On the way he updated Susan.

"Lucy told me that she had been drugged and raped by Oliver since she was ten years old. Not only that, Oliver Smith, he is her father. Oliver raped his own daughter. He did it for years. So he's probably doing it to Emily. I told Troy that I would bring Emily over so that Lucy could tell her what he'd done to her. Surely then Emily will see that she needs to terminate this pregnancy and come back home."

Susan shook her head in amazement. "Oh my God, that's disgusting, what sort of a monster is he? How could someone do that to his own child? What else has he been doing to Emily? He needs to be arrested, what is Katrina doing about it?"

"Nothing yet, she doesn't know. I want Lucy to talk to Emily first, then I'll tell Katrina."

They pulled up outside Oliver's house; Dwayne knocked at the front door. There was no reply. He knocked again. Still no reply.

He started to walk around to the back of the house. He opened the gate, and as he went up to the back door, he noticed chairs drawn up around a blanket on the ground.

Dwayne knocked at the back door. There was no reply, but the door was unlocked. Both Dwayne and Susan entered Oliver's house. They instantly noticed the trail of dried blood that led through the kitchen to the lounge. As they walked into the lounge, they could see that the sofa, which had once been light beige coloured suede, was smothered in blood. His heart sank—what had happened here and where the hell was Emily?

He pulled his phone from his jeans and dialed 000; it was answered immediately. Dwayne relayed the address and explained what he had found. He asked to be put through to Katrina urgently. The call centre was based in Sydney so it took a couple of minutes to redirect the call to Katrina.

"Clairemont Island Police, how may I help you?"

"Katrina, it's Dwayne Olsen and I'm at Oliver Smith's house. The place is covered in blood and we can't find Emily. I think something terrible has happened." Dwayne tried to keep his composure.

"Dwayne, it's OK. She's at the medical centre, and I just left Oliver's house. Emily is fine, no need to worry about her. Scotty will update you if you go to the medical centre," she said.

"Katrina, Lucy told me that Oliver had been drugging and raping her since she was ten years old. She was really distraught, but I want her to tell Emily, I'm hoping that Emily will listen to her," Dwayne pleaded.

"I've got a couple of things I need to do at the resort; can you hang around the medical centre till I get there? We'll discuss it then, OK?" said Katrina.

"OK, see you soon." Dwayne felt for sure this was going to work out for all of them; he just had to wait for Katrina to arrive. They would confront Lucy and then arrest Oliver. For the first time in ages, Dwayne felt a shimmer of hope.

Dwayne and Susan drove to the medical centre in silence, both trying to make sense of what was happening. They walked in the door, asked to speak to Scotty and sat down to wait. Scotty turned up about ten minutes later. He took them into one of the treatment rooms where Emily was waiting.

"Are you OK; we saw all that blood and wondered what happened to you?" Susan asked.

They could tell she was not quite herself. Emily was almost catatonic. She seemed incapable of speaking.

"Yes, she's fine," Scotty responded. "She took something to numb the pain of what she'd seen and heard."

"What has happened? There was so much blood in the house, has Oliver been hurt? Has someone attacked Oliver?

Did Emily see what happened, is that's what wrong with her?" Susan was panicking.

Her line of questioning was interrupted as Katrina walked into the treatment room "Dwayne, I'm going around to see Lucy. If you'd like to join me, I'm not sure she's going to be able to offer any solutions, but at least we can speak to her."

"We need to make sure Oliver is arrested for this; he needs to be held accountable for what he's done to Emily," Susan pleaded.

"That might be difficult. Oliver is missing, Susan; chances are he could be dead. We can listen to what Lucy has to say, but it's her word against his, and if he's not around to defend himself, then it's just hearsay," Katrina added.

"As soon as Emily is discharged, Susan, I want you to take her home. Put her to bed, but stay with her. Please don't let her out of your sight, she's extremely vulnerable and I don't know what she's capable of. Dwayne, come with me and we'll see what Lucy has to say. I can't promise I can do anything with it—you do understand, don't you?"

Susan drove Emily home in Dwayne's car and settled her into bed. She then made herself a pot of tea and sat in the French provincial wing-backed chair that she had bought for Emily's twelfth birthday. Emily had seen one like it on TV and begged Susan to get one for her bedroom. In all honesty, it was probably one of the most comfortable chairs in the house. Susan brought her paperwork in from the office so that she could work while Emily slept.

She spent the first hour glancing over at Emily, making sure she was still breathing. Funny, she thought, she hadn't done that since Emily had her tonsils removed when she was six. That seemed like such a long time ago; so much had happened to them all since then. Way too much. If only she could wave a magic wand and turn everything back to when they were a happy family, but in truth she didn't know when that was. How could she change it, how could she repair this, could they be saved or was it too late?

It was around two in the afternoon when Katrina and Dwayne knocked on Troy and Lucy's front door. Troy answered and showed them inside. He offered them a drink, which they refused.

"Could we speak to Lucy, please?" Katrina asked.

"I'd love to say yes, but she's not here."

"Is she at work?"

"No," Troy responded.

"Do you know when she will be back?"

"No."

"May I ask where she is?"

"I don't know where she is. She left here sometime overnight. I don't know when, but she wasn't here when I woke up," Troy reluctantly shared.

"When we went to bed, she was really distraught after revealing what had happened to her as a kid. Dwayne knows how bad she was; he was here. We climbed into bed around 9:30 p.m. and I know she tossed and turned for a while. When I woke up around 6:30 a.m. she wasn't in the bed; her side was cold, her keys were gone and so was her car. I don't know where she is, or where she could have gone, but I am starting to get worried," Troy said.

"I drove around and eventually found her car parked at the far end of the beach. I got out and walked back and forth, from one end of the beach to the other, I checked the lighthouse and the pier. I walked into every cafe and restaurant along the esplanade, but nobody has seen her. It was then I wondered if she had jumped on the ferry."

Troy wished he had called Katrina earlier that morning. This revelation had taken its toll on Lucy. Telling them about the rape was devastating for her; he could tell she was having great difficulty in sharing that. But he knew it was revealing the fact that Oliver was her father—that was what really knocked the breath out of her. That was when she mentally and physically collapsed.

He had not been entirely honest with Katrina; he failed to mention that the small bags of cocaine that she had grasped firmly in her hands were gone. He couldn't find them in the house and wondered if Lucy had flushed them down the toilet, or if she had taken them with her. He wondered if she had left the house to do something stupid; had she intended to take them in order to cause an overdose? He hoped like hell he was way off track, but he also knew she wasn't thinking clearly.

He agreed to call Katrina if he heard from her.

CHAPTER TWENTY

What Have You Done?

It was 6:00 p.m. when Lucy parked outside the home she shared with Troy, unlocked the front door and headed to the bathroom, where she promptly locked the door behind her. Troy had been out looking for her again and was surprised to see her car in the driveway when he pulled up at home. He quickly called Katrina, "She's home."

"Excellent, I'll be around soon."

He heard music playing, he tried the bathroom door, but it was locked. He knocked.

"Lucy, are you OK? I've been worried sick about you."

She didn't respond. He kept on knocking.

"Lucy, what are you doing in there?"

There was no response.

"Please unlock the door."

Still there was no response, Troy was starting to panic.

"Unlock the door now, or I swear to God I'll kick the bloody door in!"

"What's all the fuss?" she answered.

"I've been worried sick about you. Let me in, I want to know you're OK," he urged.

"I'll be out in a minute; can you pour me a glass of wine?" she asked.

Troy went to pour the wine. Katrina arrived a few minutes later. She was waiting with Troy as Lucy walked into the kitchen, looking as fresh as a daisy.

"Where the hell have you been, I've been worried sick?"

"I was at the beach," she lied.

"No! You weren't at the beach; I have been down there twice today looking for you."

"What does it matter? I'm here now."

Katrina had been silent, just watching what was unfolding between them. She wasn't even sure that Lucy knew she was there. Katrina couldn't put her finger on it, but she knew something was not quite right with Lucy.

As Troy went to embrace her. Lucy flinched and pulled away. Troy didn't notice it, but Katrina did. She suspected Lucy was not being entirely truthful.

"Lucy, could you please make me a cup of tea?" Katrina asked.

"What?" Lucy was taken aback.

"A cup of tea, could I have a cup of tea please?" Katrina repeated her question.

"OK." Lucy tried to rise from her seat, but couldn't gather the strength to do so.

"Lucy, are you OK, have you been injured?" Katrina asked.

"NO! I'm fine," Lucy snapped back.

"Then I'd like a cup of tea, please."

After a couple of attempts, Lucy managed to get up out of her chair; her slow deliberate movements answered Katrina's assumption.

"Lucy, could you please raise your top, I'd like to see your arms and torso." Katrina could tell from the way Lucy was moving that she'd done some damage; the question was to what extent and how did she sustain the injuries.

"No, I will not show you anything, I want you to leave now." Lucy's raised voice was strained; the exertion involved in doing so caused her considerable pain.

"Put it this way, Lucy, you can either show me now or I will take you to the medical centre where Scotty will be forced to examine you. Either way, I will find out the extent of your injuries. If you are in as much pain as I suspect, then you will need to see Scotty anyway."

By now Troy was really worried. What was Lucy trying to hide? Was she hurt and how did it happen, had she been in an accident? The car didn't appear to have any damage.

Lucy reluctantly raised her top—the bruising was starting to show. Katrina could tell she had been beaten, but who was capable of doing this kind of damage? Katrina hoped and prayed she was wrong in her suspicions.

"Troy, can I talk to Lucy privately, please?"

"No way. I won't leave; she needs my support."

"If you stay then you are to remain quiet, OK?"

"OK," Troy agreed as he held Lucy's hand.

"Lucy, what time did you leave here last night?"

"I don't know, I couldn't sleep; probably around 10:00 p.m."

"Where did you go when you left here?" Katrina asked.

"I needed some fresh air and went down to the beach."

"Did you see anyone? Did you talk to anyone?"

"No. Nobody."

"So, you didn't see anybody from the time you left here until you came back, is that what you are telling me?

"Yes."

"That's around fourteen hours. You said you went to the beach: what part of the beach did you go to?

"I parked at the beach, down by the lighthouse, cos it's

more sheltered, and I sat on the beach to clear my mind," her labored breath forced her to stop talking.

"What did you do while you were there?"

"Nothing, I wanted to clear my mind."

"How long did you stay there?"

"I'm not sure," she croaked.

"Are you sure you didn't see or talk to anyone?"

She shook her head.

Katrina knew she was lying. Lucy's body language spoke volumes. "What if I was to say that someone saw you on the beach and you weren't alone?" Katrina was fishing, but Lucy didn't know that.

"What, who saw me?" Lucy panicked, choking on her breath. "What did they see?"

"Lucy, I think it would be better if you told me everything that happened, rather than me finding out on my own. Your involvement in this incident will come out; there is no escaping it."

Katrina watched as Lucy pondered what to do. Lucy's body language and facial expressions proved that whatever happened was traumatic for her. She was clearly torn between telling the truth and harboring a secret.

"It's OK, Lucy. I can wait until you're ready. I'm a very patient person. I am not going anywhere, so take your time. Just start at the beginning and tell me what you did when you left here last night.

Lucy started crying, sobbing through the words. Troy held her hand, offering her support.

"It cooled down and I remembered I had a jacket in the car. As I walked back along the beach I saw him; he saw me about the same time. He started walking toward me. I knew I couldn't run to the car in time, so I stood still and prayed he'd keep on walking. He yelled out that he had eyes in the back of his head and was watching me. I told him it was too late, that I had told Troy and Dwayne all about what he did to me and they were going to the authorities. He started running toward me, so I panicked and ran in the opposite direction.

"It didn't take long for him to catch me. He grabbed me by the shoulders, shaking me that hard I felt my teeth rattle. He was yelling at me, telling me I'd be sorry, that he was going to teach me a lesson for being so stupid. He hit me so hard he knocked me to the ground. I thought I was a goner, but he dragged me around the back of the lighthouse." She stopped in mid-sentence, eyes fixed firmly on the floor.

"What happened next, Lucy?"

She couldn't move her eyes from the floor, she couldn't look at Troy, it was too painful to imagine what he was thinking.

Sobbing, speaking through her tears, she continued, "He said it was payback, telling me that Troy wouldn't want me, that nobody would want me after he'd finished with me. It was then I thought he would scar my face like his own, or kill me." Her racking tears showed no signs of slowing down.

"What happened next, Lucy? It's OK, you are safe now, you can tell me what happened, you are protected."

It took a long time for her body to regain composure. Troy kept holding her hand so tightly that finger marks were indenting into her skin, but she was incapable of feeling it; she was in a different place, another realm, reliving a trauma beyond even Katrina's comprehension.

"He . . . He . . . He . . ." She stumbled over her words, "He raped me." As she pushed the words out with a vengeance, she almost felt freed from the shackles around her, giving her the courage to carry on, to finally get it all off her chest, out of her body. "The rape was so brutal I passed out with the pain. I reckon he must have thought he'd killed me, because he wasn't around when I came to. I had no idea what the time was, but I could hardly move. I was so sore I knew I couldn't go back to Troy, not like this, so I went to my Mum's. The bungalow out the back of her place is never used, so I knew I could rest up there until I could fathom out what to do about Oliver.

"I can't live like this anymore. I want to confront him, get this sorted once and for all; it's killing me." Lucy surrendered to an avalanche of tears.

Troy smothered her in a close embrace, "It's OK, I love you. This—what he's done to you – it doesn't matter. I love you, I don't care about that. I just care about you; do you understand I just care about you?" Troy couldn't contain himself any longer; he erupted into tears as he cradled her in his arms.

"I love you too, Troy. I want to marry you, but I can't, not until all this is dealt with. I can't run from it any longer. We have to nail the bastard. Can you help me?" Lucy asked Katrina.

"I certainly hope so, Lucy," Katrina prayed.

"Did anyone see you or can anyone vouch for your whereabouts?"

"No, I don't think so, why?"

"No reason, I want to take you to the medical centre to get you checked over. When I arrived here earlier, you looked refreshed, had you showered?"

"I had a bath when I came home. I wanted to wash his filth off me, why?"

"If you have washed off his DNA then it will make it harder to prove that it was him who raped you, that's all, but let's get you seen to and we can deal with that later."

Scotty met them at the entrance to the medical centre, and showed them immediately into one of the treatment rooms. He rushed her through a barrage of tests, bloods, an X-ray, Ultrasound and a CT scan. He then reported back to Katrina that Lucy had three cracked ribs that would take a few months to heal. He took swabs, but because she had bathed, he wasn't sure he'd get any DNA.

CHAPTER TWENTY-ONE

As Clear As Mud

Down at the police station, Terry and Molly were interrogated separately. Katrina and Aaron questioned Terry. Then they questioned Molly. After a couple of hours it was evident they didn't have enough to charge either of them with the abduction of the twins, the disappearance of Oliver, or the stabbing of Cameron.

"Well, that's disappointing, I thought they were involved," Katrina confided to Gabby.

"I don't trust Terry; I'd lay a million dollar bet he's hiding something, he's so smug. I know it's a long shot, but does he have form? Have you contacted the Federal Police to check him out?"

"Yes, I sent off a request earlier this morning, but it could take a few days to get a response."

"Aaron, do we have anything yet on the black Audi?"

"Yes, they just got back to me. It seems that there are three black Audi's that live on the island. Did you want to come with me when I question them? The ferry could tell me that a black Audi, license plate ANS 102 crossed into Clairemont Island two days ago. It returned to Sydney on the first ferry crossing today. It's using false plates," Aaron reported.

"I wonder if there is a connection between this Audi, and the abduction of the twins? Let's not forget the Asian man Sean saw in the café the night we followed Oliver, they certainly knew each other. When the Asian man left the café he got into a black Audi. I was too far away to catch the license plate; I wonder if it's the same car?" Katrina pondered.

"But for now it looks like we don't have anything on Terry or Molly to hold them, so we had better let them go. When we have a body, the outcome may be different, but for now they are free to go," Katrina said.

Gabby drove them back to the resort, asking how the photo shoot was going. They were pretty tight lipped—Gabby couldn't decide whether it was a guilt thing, or if they weren't prepared to say anything on the grounds it might incriminate them.

Back in their hotel room Terry picked up the phone to call head office. He wasn't sure if Cameron had called them the night before. There was no stopping Terry now; it was a clear case of save your own arse.

His intention was to save his and Molly's jobs, by doing whatever it took.

"You need to tell head office that this is all Cameron's fault, that we had nothing to do with it, and don't forget to tell them that he disobeyed everything you told him to do." Molly was onto her third glass of wine, it was evident she wasn't thinking clearly.

"He needs to be fired for what he's done," Molly screeched from the bedroom.

"Honestly, Molly, as if you weren't to blame for some of it." Terry regretted saying it, but he couldn't take it back.

"What do you mean, I am to blame? I didn't do anything wrong, it was those bloody twins; they stuffed this whole shoot up. If you don't tell head office that, then I will."

"For Christ sake, Molly, shut up, or you'll end up getting us both fired. I don't want to hear a peep out of you while I'm speaking to them, do you hear me?"

Molly started crying. Terry was incapable of registering how vulnerable she was.

"Don't speak to me like that, Terry, I don't deserve it."

"Molly, I want you to go and have a bath, leave me alone so I can call head office and try to keep our jobs. Do you understand how serious this whole situation is?"

Molly nodded as she grabbed her glass of wine and retreated to the bathroom.

She was doing his head in; he didn't see their relationship continuing after they returned to LA.

The call to head office was easier than he had expected. They didn't seem to care about all the in-house bickering, just as long as the company's reputation had not been tarnished.

Head office was really impressed with the photos Cameron had been sending them.

"What's the story with Molly, how come I haven't seen her in any of the photos recently?" Sandy, head editor of the magazine asked.

"She was injured the other night and Cameron wouldn't photograph her. He said that makeup didn't conceal it enough, but that's a matter of opinion. He wouldn't use her in the shoot the following day either."

"Is she OK? How badly is she hurt and, more importantly, how did she get injured?"

"One of the models told her she had a fat arse, and they got into a fight. Yes, she's OK, just some bruises and a cut lip. Her ego took the biggest battering."

"OK, I understand. But you're saying that Cameron won't

use her and makeup won't cover it?"

"Yeah, that about sums it up."

"Do you not agree with his judgment?" Sandy asked.

"Not entirely. I believe he has an ulterior motive."

"What do you think he's up to?"

"Look, I can't prove anything; just know that we haven't agreed on many things here."

"I'm really impressed with the talent he's using; I love how their energy oozes off the page. Stunning talent, impeccable photos and the locations are beyond anything I could have imagined, but if you like I'll have a chat to him." Sandy suggested.

"That may be difficult. He seems to have gone missing. The police are searching for him. I'll let you know as soon I as get an update," a deflated Terry told her.

"What do you mean, he's gone missing? What's going on over there? Is the rest of the crew OK?"

"Yes, everyone else is OK. I'll update you when I hear something, OK?"

At the medical centre Cameron started to come around. "Well hello, Mr. Collins, I trust you are feeling better?" Scotty asked.

"Where am I, what happened?" Cameron asked.

"You are in Clairemont Medical Centre, I'm Dr. Scott and you were stabbed. You are extremely lucky; this injury could have been fatal, as it nicked the brachial artery, but your bicep muscle took the biggest hit. You lost a lot of blood and we have given you a transfusion. You will be OK; but the arm will take a long time to heal. We will keep you in for a few days. I'll have to see how you recuperate, but I don't think you'll be able to fly back to Los Angeles as anticipated. Do you have any questions?" Scotty asked.

"Who stabbed me? Is everyone else OK?"

"The twins are OK, just shocked at what happened. We

haven't been able to find Oliver though, are you up to talking to the police? They need a statement from you."

"Not sure what I can say to them. I don't know anything, I'm not even sure I saw anything. Oliver told us to run, to get away. It was his tone of voice that made us realise he wasn't fooling and that we'd better move fast. The door to the bedroom was open and I pushed the twins into there, hoping it had a lock on the door. Everything is kinda hazy. I don't remember much else."

"Rest up now, I'll let Detective Inspector Reid know you are awake and she'll pop over to see you soon." Scotty added as he went to call Katrina.

Fifteen minutes later Katrina closed the door to Cameron's room. She sat down beside him and waited for him to wake up.

"Hello, Mr. Collins, I'm Detective Inspector Reid. Can I ask a couple of questions about the incident that happened in your room?"

"As I said to the doctor, I'm not sure I can be of any help. I didn't see anyone."

"Firstly, can you tell me how you know Oliver Smith?"

"I met him on the ferry on the way over, he told me about all the wonderful places on the island to photograph. I was so impressed with his generosity I asked him over for drinks."

"Can you confirm who was in your room at the time of the incident?"

"Myself, the twins and Oliver, that's all."

"Do you have any idea who may have wanted to harm the twins?

"No."

"Do you know anything about their abduction from Grandberry Estate? Did they mention anyone who may want to harm them?"

"No, but I wouldn't put it past Terry or Molly to do

something like that. Molly had it out for the twins; they had fought the day before."

"Yes, I know about that. In all the time you have worked with Terry and Molly, do you really feel they are capable of following through with this kind of attack?"

"I'm not sure. They were really angry, but no, they're basically gutless."

"Thank you. I have no further questions for now, but I may come back later."

As Katrina was leaving the medical centre, Gabby turned up with Katy and Anton.

"Hello, Mr. Collins, sorry to hear of your accident. Please let the resort know if you require anything while you're in here. I hope you don't mind, but housekeeping has packed all your things and moved them into a new room. Let the resort know when you are to be discharged and we will come and pick you up and show you to your new room," Gabby explained.

With a heavy heart he finally replied, "That's OK."

"I also have a message here for you from LA," she said as she handed him an envelope.

"Thanks for dropping us off, Ms Saintclaire. We'll make our own way back to the resort," Katy told Gabby.

As soon as Gabby left the room, Katy and Anton raced over to Cameron and sat down.

"Oh my God, are you OK? We've been worried sick about you. We thought you'd been killed. They told us that your room was a crime scene, that it was covered in blood. What happened?" Katy asked.

"I'm not sure; the twins turned up after they escaped from being tied up in the boot of a car at Grandberry Estate. We were having a few quiet drinks with a guy I'd met on the ferry when he saw someone outside my room. He told us to run, and to meet back at his place. Seems he must have known who it was, because he sounded really scared. We ran into the bedroom, at some point I got stabbed. Hell, I didn't even realise this guy had made it into the room. Everything happened so fast I didn't have time to think. The rest is pretty fuzzy, I kept drifting in and out of consciousness, but I remember hearing fighting and feeling the coldness of the bathtub. I don't know how long we stayed there, then I woke up and I was here."

"Jez, that's terrible," Katy stated.

"We thought Terry and Molly had done something to you, the way things have been lately. They were acting really strange at the estate; it made all of us think they had something to do with the twin's disappearance. I honestly wouldn't put it past them," Katy said.

"Yeah, I thought of that as well, especially yesterday, as every time I looked over at them they just seemed so smug, like they had something to hide."

"I told the copper lady that you two had been at each other's throats for days. Then I saw them take Terry and Molly away. I don't know if they are still at the police station. We've been waiting for an update on them. Gabby told us you were in here and we could come and see you."

"Oh well, it's in the hands of the police, so if they've done something I assume the coppers will figure it out. At least you are safe and the twins are OK."

After they left, Cameron remembered the envelope; he tore it open and read the message.

It was from Dr. Stamos, from Huntington Hospital in Pasadena. He quickly dialed the number and was told by the emergency room doctor that his fiancée, Anthea Stevens, had been seriously injured in a car accident three days ago. Unfortunately, she had passed away a few hours earlier.

Cameron sobbed into his hospital gown. What have I done? he thought. I was so angry with her that I deliberately cheated on her, but all this time she has been lying in a hospital bed, fighting for her last breath. This is my fault, I have caused everything that has happened here—the twins getting abducted, and now Anthea's death—it's all my fault. He continued to weep.

He tried to sleep, but he knew he was fooling himself; chances were he'd never sleep again.

CHAPTER TWENTY-TWO

A Glimmer of Hope

Katrina pulled up outside the Olsen home; she noticed Dwayne's car parked in the driveway. Susan escorted Katrina inside, where she found Dwayne at the kitchen table.

"Are you here to see Emily?" Dwayne asked.

"Yesterday was such a crazy day. I wanted to check up on Emily, and get a statement from her."

"She's still sleeping. I was just about to make coffee; would you like one?" Susan asked Katrina.

"Yes, please, that would be lovely."

"I'm sorry to have to ask, Dwayne, but where were you between 11:00 p.m. and 8:00 a.m.?" Katrina asked.

"At the medical centre. I came here to check up on Emily. Susan and I sat down and talked about everything that happened over the last few days; we were still in shock. We didn't realise that Emily had gotten out of bed and was standing behind us listening. When we talked about what Oliver had done to Lucy, we heard her scream.

"She told us we were making it up, that Lucy was lying.

She was clearly traumatised. It took ages to settle her down again. I was going to go home, but Susan asked if I would stay to keep her company, as she was really worried about Emily.

"Two hours later, Emily started screaming again. We ran into her bedroom where we saw all this blood in her bed. I picked her up and rushed her to the medical centre."

"Is she OK? What was wrong with her?" Katrina asked.

"She had a miscarriage. Seems that all the stress about Oliver caused her to miscarry," Dwayne answered.

"As terrible as that is in itself, it's a good thing though, don't you think?" Katrina cautiously inquired.

"We think so, but we're not sure Emily will ever see the logic of it," Susan said.

"We both stayed the night at the medical centre. She had a D&C this morning and we only just got back home. I presume she will sleep for a few hours; I definitely don't want to wake her. Maybe you could come back later to get the statement?" Susan suggested.

"Yes, that's OK, I'll pop back later."

Katrina went back to the station. She was no further ahead with her investigations.

Oliver was still missing. His mobile was not registered with any service provider, therefore he was probably using a burner phone, which certainly didn't help them to identify who he called or, more importantly, who called him. He had not reported for work and the ferry crew had not seen him. He had not returned to his home. Katrina had informed Sydney and they were going to broadcast his description on television Australia-wide.

The twins' abduction was still unsolved and, although Katrina and Aaron had personally talked to them, the three Audi owners on the island could all account for their whereabouts and they didn't appear to raise any suspicion.

The black Audi that travelled back to Sydney had false license plates. The security cameras in the ferry terminal and on the ferry were not working that morning and the terminal staff had no account as to why.

Lucy had spent the night at the medical centre—Scotty was genuinely concerned for her wellbeing. He had not seen a rape like that on the island before. Through the heavy bleeding he could identify there was a lot of internal damage. She was heavily sedated, but he wanted to take her to theatre to examine her fully. From what he could see, he suspected she may need a hysterectomy, but he could wait until she was in a position to fully understand the consequence of that discussion. For now, she was relatively stable.

Katrina dropped in to see Lucy's mother. Yes, there was a bungalow out the back, but it looked relatively undisturbed. Had Lucy really spent the night there? If Lucy had passed out on the beach, then how could she have known where Oliver was going? She wouldn't know.

Did Lucy have the strength to confront Oliver twice in one night? If the rape had occurred on the beach, of which Katrina could find no substantial proof, if Lucy indeed needed to recuperate in her mother's bungalow for fourteen hours, then she could not have been at Cameron's room. And why would Lucy stab Cameron? She had no motive to attack anyone other than Oliver. Did Lucy have the strength to carry out a full-blown attack on Oliver and live to tell the tale? Lucy may be relatively tall, but she's only a size 6. Oliver could push her over with his little finger. Plus, how would she dispose of his body by herself? Katrina felt confident that Lucy couldn't take Oliver on and win.

Katrina had nothing on Terry or Molly; they had no cuts, bruises or any fight-related injuries. If they'd gone into that room with Oliver, chances were they would be supporting serious injuries. Katrina couldn't prove they had anything to do with the twins' abduction, Cameron's stabbing or Oliver's disappearance. Therefore, she had no choice but to allow them to leave the island. They were warned that if a body was found they were to make themselves available for more interviews.

The crew called in to the medical centre to say goodbye to Cameron; he was not allowed to travel for at least another week.

As the magazine crew stood on the deck of the Clairemont ferry, they looked back at the island with mixed emotions. The crew that had arrived on the island ten days earlier were not the same people who departed today. Life had caused them to question not only themselves, but also the nature of humanity.

Terry had kept head office updated on Cameron's condition. Thanks to him they had three award winning photos. The in-house bickering was not talked about again. The distance between Terry and Molly was evident to the crew, but nobody cared about them being an item. It was a secret that would stay on the island. There was no mention that anyone would lose their jobs. Head office wasn't interested; they had what they wanted, front covers that would make them millions.

Joan was on duty at front reception when Hōne arrived back at the resort. "How are you enjoying your holiday, Mr. Parkes?"

"It's brilliant, thanks, and you know what? I'm seriously thinking of staying on. I feel it's exactly where I need to be right now. Is there any chance you can hook me up with a really good realtor? I think I'd like to rent for a while. I have nothing to get back to Sydney for and the sea change would be good for me."

"I know just the person. I can organise that for you, if you like? Do you have a time frame for when you would like to go out looking?" Joan asked.

"I'm easy, any time is good for me," he answered.

Back at the police station, Katrina was feeling deflated. What was she missing? She glanced at Gabby and Aaron for encouragement, but nothing. As they scrunched their shoulders in defeat, the outlook was not promising.

"We did take Oliver's fingerprints when we arrested him, didn't we?" Katrina asked Aaron.

"Yes, of course. I put him through the database, but he's not in the system, why?" Aaron asked.

"Just to make sure we've eliminated that line of inquiry. I remember when I checked the ferry crew through the system he didn't come up, but I wondered if his fingerprints unlocked anything. I'd really love to know where he came from before here, but I couldn't find any personal papers at his house, there weren't any photos, not even a passport."

"Why don't you ask the HR manager for the ferry to provide his personnel file? That should include an address for when he started. His letter of offer would most definitely have his previous address." Gabby suggested.

"Great idea. In fact, I already have his personnel file. They supplied that a month ago when I first started doing surveillance on them," she told them as she pulled their files from the filing cabinet. "Here is Oliver's letter of offer. Aaron can you please get me the number for The Matador Hotel in Phillip Bay," Katrina asked as she continued to read the rest of Oliver's personnel file.

"No reply, I'll keep trying," Aaron interrupted their conversation.

"A hotel, I would ask them to provide you with the address he used when he first registered. Hotels always ask for an address, back then some even requested your car licence plate," Gabby recalled.

"OK, so the reason I'm not getting a reply is because of

this," he said as he turned his computer screen around for them to see a newspaper heading: '4th May 2000 Fire engulfs The Matador Hotel.' He read the rest of the article out loud: "A 'May the 4th be with you' party ends in disaster as twenty of its residents and guests perished in the lobby of the hotel. It was reported an explosion was heard, but it's yet to be determined if the explosion occurred before or after the fire'."

"Bummer, there goes another lead."

Would the mystery of the last few days ever be uncovered? There were plenty of people who certainly hoped so, but without a body, it was certainly challenging. Katrina was at a dead end. She leafed through the paperwork looking for possible leads they had overlooked, but nothing jumped out.

"I reckon we might have to call it a night and look over this again with fresh eyes," she indicated.

"Sounds like a plan. Michael will be wondering where I am, it's been five hours since I left the resort. Aaron, can I drive you back to the resort?" Gabby asked.

"If that's OK with you, Katrina. I'd like an early night so that I'm refreshed in the morning and Storm needs to be fed," Aaron responded.

Katrina nodded in agreement as both Gabby and Aaron walked out of the police station. She didn't intend to leave yet, just one more glance at the notes before she called it a night, she wouldn't be long. She looked at the clock on the wall; it was 8:00 p.m. If I haven't found anything by 10:00 p.m. I will go home she instructed herself. It was then her mobile rang. She checked the screen to see who would be calling her at this time of the night, and was pleased to see it was Sean.

"Hi, Sean, how is everything in Sydney?" Katrina asked.

"All good here, but how are you getting on over there? With Aaron seconded, you should be able to get a handle on the drug situation. Do you know yet if Oliver is the only supplier or have you uncovered more leads?"

"No, sorry to say we're at a dead end. Oliver only had enough for recreational use, so I don't know for certain, my gut tells me that he is, but without proof the jury's is still out."

"I've got heaps of leave; did you want me to come over for a week to help out? I'd love the distraction and even though I'd be off duty, I could still help brainstorm and we could do some undercover work. Keep Aaron in uniform and me out of uniform, the locals wouldn't know any different."

"My gut says yes, but only if you promise to observe and be a third pair of eyes and ears, then I'd love to have you. I don't want you getting in trouble with head office," Katrina found it refreshing to actually smile, thinking she hadn't done much smiling all day.

"I'll see you tomorrow. Not sure yet which ferry I will cross over on; I do have a couple of things to tidy up before I come over. I'll let you know."

"Sounds like a plan, and thanks so much, you're one in a million." Katrina was secretly pleased they had become friends way back on recruit training at the academy.

"Oh, I forgot. I was also ringing to double check the licence plate for the black Audi. I want to do a few more searches."

"The plate on the black Audi that crossed the morning of the incident was ANS 102," Katrina responded.

"Thanks, I'll let you know if I uncover anything," Sean told her as he said his goodbye and hung up.

She forgot to ask if he wanted to stay with her. She assumed he would, but then remembered the state of her house. Looking at the paperwork on her desk she decided to pack it up. I'd better clean the house before Sean arrives, she thought.

The house she rented was only a short block from the police station; convenience was the reason behind renting it, as opposed to the feel or layout of the house. She'd never actually thought of it as her home. It didn't feel homelike, just a place to sleep: that was all she was after. Five minutes later she let herself into her modest two-bedroom bungalow. She cleaned the kitchen bench, dropped the few dirty dishes into the dishwasher and turned that on while she went to scrub the bathroom and change the sheets in the spare room. A quick vacuum and she poured herself a glass of wine to enjoy as she watched the floor dry.

All the time her mind was on the case. Over and over, thoughts raced through her mind. She started with each suspect and walked their means, motive, opportunity and then their alibi through her filter process. Over her years on the Force she had used this process many times with great success. When she was confident with her findings she would download it with specifics. So far everything mapped out, but it didn't stop her from mulling it over once more.

Dwayne had been removed from the equation, he definitely had means and motive, but he did not have the opportunity. She had personally called the medical centre and they had confirmed Emily, Dwayne and Susan had spent the night, none of them had left the centre, Dwayne was in the clear. She would of course visit Emily the next day to make sure she was OK. Also, to let Dwayne and Susan know that she was not going to pursue any charges with Emily regarding drug use, as long as Emily was forthcoming with information on where Oliver got his supply from or who he dealt to. She had no proof yet of his involvement with trafficking, but her intuition and gut reaction was that he had more to reveal on the distribution of drugs on the island. The seven thousand dollars in petty cash he had stored in his safe told her a different story. She anticipated that he had shared some of that information with Emily, and that Emily was now possibly scared enough to divulge what she knew. Katrina certainly hoped so.

She didn't trust Terry, but unfortunately, she had confirmation from the federal police that he was squeaky clean, so even though that was not how Katrina felt about him, she had to respect their findings.

Molly was in the clear, her tiny size 6 frame could not have implicated her in any aggravated assault either on the twins or Cameron. She would have needed help and in Katrina's honest opinion Terry didn't have the guts to follow through with anything violent, even though she didn't trust him. She knew there was something untoward with Terry, she just couldn't lay her finger on it.

That left Lucy. All the evidence pointed toward Lucy being in the clear, but her gut told her there was something different going on with Lucy. Katrina wasn't sure if what Lucy was hiding was part of the case or something else. Katrina would have to wait. Lucy was not well enough to speak, and she'd already identified that Troy knew nothing about her past.

Oliver was still missing. Who was responsible? What provoked the attack, was it drugs or some other issue? Where was he? Where was the perp? How did they disappear? If Katrina could answer these questions then she could move forward with the case.

The clock clicked midnight. This is ridiculous, Katrina thought, I have to get some sleep. She respected Gabby, they hadn't actually worked together while they were both based in Sydney but she was aware of Gabby's reputation and Gabby had a 100% success rate for all her cases. She took a moment as she prepared herself for bed to think what Gabby would do right now in this case. Where would her head be, what gut instincts would she be following?

At 3:00 a.m. Katrina woke, she wasn't sure why. Was it a noise that woke her? She lay in bed eyes wide open listening to the energy of the house, listening to the outside creaks as the wind danced around the wooden bungalow. It was in that moment the wind, or something, spoke to her. "*All is not what it seems*." The words echoed through her head.

"What does that even mean?" she asked herself.

She closed her eyes and listened; what else could she hear in the whisper of the atmosphere? She listened harder, more intently, but nothing. Not a thing followed those few words. OK, so what did it mean? *All is not what it seems*. She already knew that. She had already pondered who was responsible for the disappearance of Oliver and the attack on Cameron. She had already wondered what had transpired in Cameron's room. More than once she had contemplated the possibility that the body of Oliver would appear, so that she could solve this crime.

The *why* was almost a no brainer. Katrina firmly believed it was drug related. She believed that Oliver was dealing, and she almost believed that Emily was mixed up in it. Perhaps the twins were too, otherwise why were they abducted, why were they singled out, who did it and why did that person leave them in the boot of the Audi and not drive them out of Grandberry Estate at the time? Why leave them there?

In relation to Oliver, there were way too many questions. Assuming the body wrapped in the bedspread had been dragged to a car in the car park, where did the car then drive to? Storm had followed a scent to the ferry. Had the car already returned to Sydney or was that a diversion? Who was dragged in the bedspread, was it Oliver or the perp? It would have taken a person of strength to attack and fight Oliver, especially if the twins were correct in their assumption that the fight went on for quite some time and sounded vicious? That kind of attack would have been instigated by someone of great strength, definitely not a petite size 6 woman. Who is missing from the equation? Who has slipped through the radar? Someone else must be involved, but who? Or maybe there was more than one perp, she hadn't thought about that scenario. That in itself raised a dozen questions. She had a lot to worry about as she forced sleep.

CHAPTER TWENTY-THREE

Some Movement Forward

Katrina was woken by her alarm, but only just before Gabby rang her. "Morning. I had the worst sleep ever. I kept thinking about that Audi and the Asian man in Sydney. If we assume Oliver was meeting him in a quest for drugs that night in Sydney, and the twins were dumped into the boot of an Audi in the carpark of Grandberry Estate. How would the driver or Asian man, if that's who we suspect, know the twins would be there for the photo shoot? Remember they were a last minute add on. Nobody knew they would be there, not even the magazine crew. The Audi must have been following them. That is the only reason I can think of to link them all together, if they are in fact connected," Gabby blurted.

"I hadn't thought of that scenario, good thinking." Katrina said.

"I'll go down to the ferry this morning to see if I can get any of the crew to talk about Oliver. Surely someone will spill the beans, and come clean about his dealings; someone must have seen what he gets up to in Sydney."

Gabby nodded in approval, "Sounds like a plan, but personally, I would put the squeeze on Emily, get her to come clean about her involvement with drugs. She must know more than she's letting on. Paint a different picture of Oliver for her, something that fills her with doubt and fear. You should get the support of her parents; they want this uncovered just as much as we do," Gabby continued.

"Did you want to come with me to see them?" Katrina asked.

"I do, but Michael is tightening the screws on me. If you let me know what time, I'll try, but no promises."

"I'll head into the office soon, so I can be ready to visit them at 8:00 a.m. Will that work?" Katrina inquired.

"Should be OK, I'll tell Michael I'm off to the supermarket." It's a little white lie, but who cares? Gabby lied to herself.

Katrina put a bottle of wine in the fridge to chill before cleaning up her breakfast dishes. There wasn't anything exciting to eat in the house, but that didn't matter. There were plenty of places to eat along the promenade or at the resort. Satisfied that it looked perfect, she acknowledged her hard work last night. She took one last look around her modest bungalow as she locked the door. She wasn't sure what time Sean would arrive, but she now knew she was ready for him whenever he turned up.

She had enough time to check her emails, and assign Aaron some work before picking Gabby up at the resort and heading over to Susan's house. She hoped to catch Susan before she headed to work. The real estate office didn't open until 9:00 a.m. and Dwayne definitely didn't start work at the supermarket until 9:00 a.m. Even if she was up to it after her D & C the other day, Emily would not leave for school until 8:45 a.m. for a 9:00 a.m. start. Katrina was confident they would all still be at home.

Gabby stood in front of Katrina as she knocked on the door. Dwayne's car was parked outside, so that was a good omen. They must have resolved some of their past, which would be a great thing. Gabby was pleased about that. She remembered way back before Susan's affair with Lenni and Grant, back to the days when Dwayne and Susan were a couple, happier times when they attended parties at the resort, those were the times that her thoughts lingered on. Well, until the door was answered by a distraught Susan rubbing her bloodshot eyes.

"Is everything OK?" Gabby was genuinely concerned.

"Yes, but Emily is taking this whole thing worse than I'd have anticipated. Neither Dwayne nor I can get her to see reason. She is adamant Oliver never touched her and that Lucy is lying. She is accusing Lucy of ruining Oliver's reputation. She just won't see reason."

"Can we speak to Emily, maybe we can say something to make her see sense?" Gabby certainly hoped so.

"Yes, please, but only if you promise not to aggravate her any more than she already is."

"I can't promise anything, but I will try my best to get her to see Oliver for who he really is. However, it will be confronting for her," Katrina responded honestly.

"She's in her room; I'll go and get her. Would you like a cup of tea?" Susan asked.

"That would be nice, thank you." Gabby nodded as she and Katrina seated themselves at the table with Dwayne.

"How are you holding up?" Gabby asked Dwayne.

"I'm good, thanks. Obviously I'm concerned for Emily, but we are putting on a united front," he said as he looked at Susan and smiled.

"I'm pleased about that, she will need all your support, and to know you are united will be of great comfort to her right now," Gabby said as she placed her hand on his shoulder.

Dwayne finished making their tea as Susan escorted Emily into the kitchen.

"Emily, I'm really sorry to hear of your emergency the other night, it must have been frightening for you," Katrina said.

Emily nodded. Katrina could tell she was struggling to form the words to describe how she felt.

"I want you to think back to that night when the twins and Cameron came to Oliver's house. It must have been confronting for you to have them come barging in on you. Can you remember what happened or recall anything they said?" Katrina asked. She wanted Emily to know she was aware that Emily had lost the baby, but didn't want to dwell on it: she wasn't going to let Emily side-line this discussion. No, this discussion had to be about Oliver and drugs.

"Emily, I'm sorry, but I have to get a statement from you about what happened at Oliver's house the other night. I know it might be uncomfortable remembering what happened, but it's important we understand what occurred from your point of view, do you understand?"

"Yes, as long as it helps find Oliver," she sobbed.

Gabby wrote the statement as Katrina coached Emily to remember everything from the time she had arrived at Oliver's house until the time Katrina and Gabby arrived. Emily struggled to look at her parents as she mentioned smoking marijuana. Katrina then got Gabby to read the statement back to Emily before asking her to sign it. Not wanting Emily to get complacent, Katrina moved forward with more questions.

"What was his frame of mind, did you notice anything unusual or out of the ordinary?"

"No," Emily choked through her tears.

"You're going to find him, right?" Emily asked, almost pleadingly.

"We will do our best Emily, but we will need your help. Can I count on you to help us?" Katrina asked.

"Yes, of course, but how can I help?" Emily asked.

"We believe this is drug related. Do you know who Oliver gets his supply from?" Katrina could see the flash of terror in her eyes, her face had flushed and her breathing was laboured. Katrina knew she had hit a nerve, now to dig a little deeper.

"Emily, before you answer me, trust me when I say we will protect you. You can confidently tell me who it is and know that you are perfectly safe." Katrina watched her reaction and thought she saw a glimmer of hope.

"I don't know who he gets it from. I think he comes home from Sydney with it, but I'm not sure. He's never told me and to be honest I've never asked."

Katrina and Gabby both noticed she had started to fidget, wiping the outside of her nose and moving her feet from side to side. Knowing the next question may put the fear of God into her, Katrina knew she wouldn't be doing her job right if she didn't ask.

"I know you may not want to answer this, Emily, but could you please tell me if Oliver mentioned any people he may have dealings with? We know that the twins were his customers, they have told us of their part in all of this. You won't get anyone in any trouble, but we need to know who they are so that we can get a clearer picture of his movements. How did he get his supply to his customers?"

Emily took a moment to digest Katrina's' question. She didn't want to get Oliver in trouble, but she did want to find him; she hoped she was doing the right thing. "They would come to his house; they would call first and then turn up. I didn't answer his phone or the door, so I really don't know who they are, sorry about that. I thought the less I knew the better off I would be."

"Are you sure you never saw anyone you know come to his house or talk to him? Are you sure he never mentioned anyone's name?"

"No, nobody." She seemed believable.

"OK, thanks for that. At this stage we have no idea where Oliver is or what has become of him. Until we get more leads on his drug dealing we will probably never be able to uncover who is responsible for his disappearance, or for the attack on the twins and Cameron's stabbing. This is a shame because the longer it takes to get evidence, the less chance there is of solving this. Oliver could be out there bleeding to death and we wouldn't know where to find him unless someone tells us everything they know. But I won't take any more of your time, I see you are ready for school," Katrina said finally as she rose from the table.

Gabby waited until they were driving back to the resort before sharing her observations. "Interesting how her body language changed when you asked about where he gets his supply from and who he sells to. Although she seemed genuinely concerned for him and his whereabouts, she isn't yet prepared to share all her truth, but I do love your final remark. She will dwell on that all day. I'd be surprised if you don't hear back from her within a few hours."

"I saw the change too, which is why I think she'll make an appearance at the station. I think she knows more than she wants her parents to hear, which doesn't surprise me. If she doesn't come forward today then I'll deliberately bump into her tomorrow," Katrina said.

She thanked Gabby for accompanying her as she dropped her safely back at the resort, to Michael who was waiting in the lobby. "Grocery shopping were we!" he laughed, knowing his wife was not going to rest until this crime was solved, signed, sealed and delivered.

CHAPTER TWENTY-FOUR

Surprise Revelations

Sean called. "Hey Katrina, I'm going to make the morning crossing, I'm just trying to find a car park. it's pretty packed here at the ferry terminal carpark. The ferry doesn't leave for another hour but rest assured I will make it."

"Brilliant, I can't wait to see you. I know it's only been a few days but it honestly feels like forever since we spent quality time together. I made up the spare room for you. Hope that's OK, but if you'd rather stay at the resort I understand."

"I was hoping you had room for me. Oh my God, you are not going to believe this," he suddenly interrupted himself. "The black Audi, it's here, in the car park. ANS 102, correct?"

"Yes, that's it," Katrina eagerly responded.

Grabbing a pair of disposable gloves from the side compartment of his car, he pulled them onto his hands as he walked toward the black Audi. "Whoever drove it back from Clairemont Island must have just dumped it. It's not locked, but the downside is there are no surveillance cameras around this area of the car park. I'm not sure if that was planned or not," Sean said excitedly as he opened the driver door and started rummaging around, looking for any clues as to the owner or driver. "Nothing lying around, no signs of forced entry, no wires out, so the driver must have had a key. Just the usual in the glovebox: umbrella, tissues, coin purse, note pad and some pens." He popped the bonnet to get the car's vehicle identification number and relayed the seventeen characters to Katrina.

She punched it into the system. "The owner of the Audi is a Jamie Chee. He doesn't have any form, but I'll call him now."

"OK, you do that and I'll call the boys to come down and dust for prints," he replied as he opened the boot.

"Hang on! It looks like I've found your missing person," Sean reported as he gently rolled the body in the boot to view his face. "Middle aged male, approximately 80kg. His hoodie is covering most of his face, but he looks to have long hair. It's matted with blood, but would guess it's brown. Looks to me like his throat has been cut, obviously the coroner will have to identify cause of death. Does this sound like your guy?" Sean asked as Katrina breathed a sigh of relief.

"Sounds like Oliver. Does he have a scar on his face?" Katrina asked.

"Pretty much looks like it, but there is so much blood I can't say for certain. I'm not touching the face. I'll confirm that after he's been seen and photographed."

"That's a load off my mind. Are you still going to come over?" she asked.

"Absolutely. Just let me get this all sorted from this end and hopefully I can get on the last crossing tonight. I'll update you as soon as I know more," Sean said.

Katrina relayed the conversation to an eager Aaron who was hanging off her every word. She picked up the phone and called Gabby to let her know.

The important action of the moment was to call this Jamie Chee to determine if he was the rightful owner of the Audi and get a clearer picture as to its disappearance. Hoping that once they found out where the car came from, it might make it easier to pinpoint who could be responsible for the crime.

Three hours later, Katrina called Gabby back. "The Audi is registered to Jamie Chee. When he answered he was not forthcoming with any information, except to say that he was on holiday in Singapore and from what he knew his car was sitting in the long-term carpark at Sydney International airport. He's not due back until next Tuesday."

"When did he fly out?" Gabby asked.

"Two weeks ago. My theory is that the perp grabbed plates off a nearby car, probably at the airport. I imagine if its owners are still overseas, we won't hear anything until they get back."

"The date clears him of being the Asian man that Oliver met in Sydney. Jamie would already have been in Singapore. The car definitely could have been the one used that night. It seems plausible that the perp stole the car, to meet with Oliver in Sydney and then followed him to Clairemont Island, only to return the morning after the crime."

"How do the twins fit into this crime? I still can't work out how they could have been targeted and dumped into the boot of the Audi, which must be the same one that's now in the car park of the ferry terminal in Sydney. Nobody knew they would be at Grandberry Estate that day. Not unless they were followed, or unless they were in the wrong place at the wrong time," Aaron suggested.

"You're right. I think we need to bring them back in for further questioning. If we put the squeeze on them they might just give us something to work with," Katrina said as she picked up her mobile to call them into the police station.

"Hello Fay, It's Katrina here. Could you and Faith please come down to the station today?' I'd like to retrace your footsteps at Grandberry Estate and the resort. Something just doesn't add up and there may be something you have overlooked that will help us find Oliver."

"We can come down now," Fay sounded choked up, as though she'd been crying.

"Thanks, Fay, I appreciate you coming down. It's important we find Oliver as soon as possible."

"That would be good, I'm really worried about him," Fay said forcefully.

"I know. I'll see you soon," Katrina responded.

She knew it was a waste of breath, but she'd have blamed herself later, had she not mentioned to Aaron to keep the discovery of Oliver's body absolutely quiet. They would say nothing, especially to the twins and Emily, until such time as they uncovered everything they wanted to know about Oliver and his drug dealing. If they were to find out he was dead, they may think that the perp was out to get them as well, to tie up loose ends and witnesses. Either way, they would clam up tighter than a duck's backside. Funny she would think of that analogy now, it was something her father used to say all the time. For the last forty years Katrina's father was a serving member of the Melbourne police force. She wished he would retire, his health was not the best and she worried for his safety especially since he'd returned to duty after his hip replacement earlier in the year. She wondered what he would do with the information on hand, what tactic would he use with the twins and Emily? If she could crack the twins, she may just have a chance of solving this case.

She closed her eyes and took a few deep breaths, trying to quieten her mind as she waited for the twins to arrive.

Your first instinct is usually right, was another of her father's common quotes which felt right, felt timely, and was a gentle reminder to trust herself, especially now. "Thanks, Dad, I needed that," she whispered to herself.

True to their word, Fay and Faith were seated in the police station within minutes. Katrina was correct: they looked visibly shaken. Their bloodshot eyes with dark rings underneath spoke volumes and you could hear the crackle in their voices that matched their look, the look of utter despondency.

Faith was the first to speak, "We went to see Cameron again today, he still looks awful but Scotty said he is making great progress, which is good because I really thought he was going to die. I don't blame Oliver for it, but wonder if Oliver wasn't there that night, would that attack still have happened? Oliver obviously knew who it was who attacked us. Do you think it was the same person who knocked us out and threw us in the boot?"

"It certainly looks like it could be the same person, but we don't have any proof yet. Who knew you were going to be at the photo shoot at Grandberry Estate?" Katrina asked.

"Nobody, it was a last-minute thing. Cameron called us because Molly was still bruised from the fight the night before. He said he wouldn't shoot her and called us to come over for the second part of the photo shoot."

"At any time over the last few days have you felt you were followed or that someone was watching you?" Katrina asked.

"No, I don't think anyone is watching or following us. I haven't noticed anyone suspicious around, have you, Faith?" Fay asked as Faith scrunched her shoulders in reply.

"You have already acknowledged that you have bought drugs from Oliver for many years. Thanks for that, I appreciate your honesty and no, I have no intention of taking that further. I just hope that you realise the seriousness of the situation and learn from the experience.

"Do you know if anyone else on the island is dealing? Now, before you answer, I am asking only to identify if someone else is setting up on the island and trying to get Oliver out of the picture. I want to catch the perpetrator just as much as you do, but I need to know what is happening on the island in relation to drugs. This is so that I can either eliminate people or get closer to solving the disappearance of Oliver and the attack on Cameron and yourselves. Are you willing to help me to move forward?"

Katrina certainly hoped so, as now was the time to hit with all guns blazing, but she needed their help, their input. She hoped they held the key to the puzzle and she also hoped they wanted a favourable outcome just as much as she did.

Faith was the first to speak, "We wondered that ourselves. We called a few mates this arvo to get a feel for what's happening. The general consensus is that nobody is tapping into Oliver's market on the island, but I also heard that ice is doing the rounds of the school yard. I have no idea who they are getting it from because Oliver doesn't deal in ice. He's told us many times he won't supply it. Maybe Emily can shed some light on where it's coming from, but, no, it's not from Oliver."

"Do you know where Oliver scores his stock?"

"Someone in Sydney. He said that he has one shift which allows him sufficient time to get to his supplier and make it back to the ferry with enough time to board and make his final checks before sailing back to Clairemont Island, but no, he has never divulged his source."

"Thanks for your honesty; I appreciate your sticking your necks out. I have no intention of taking any of your indiscretions further. But should we meet again under different circumstances, I may not be as lenient, do you understand?"

"Yes, we do," they responded in unison.

"I will contact you if we uncover anything relevant to your attack. We may need to talk further in that case. Thank you for coming in."

Katrina watched as the twins left; she felt the wind had been knocked out of their sails and wondered if Oliver was entirely to blame for that. She busied herself with paperwork, waiting to hear from Sean as to when he would be crossing on the ferry.

She looked up to catch the time, only to see through the corner window that Emily was standing outside the building. She felt inclined to run outside and drag her in, but she knew full well for this to work Emily had to be a willing participant. Emily had to want the outcome more than Katrina. She wasn't sure if Emily could see her through the window or not, so she lowered her gaze and continued with her paperwork, secretly praying that Emily would enter of her own free will. Thankfully, some ten minutes later, Emily sheepishly walked through the front door of the police station. Katrina, aware of her presence, ignored her first reaction to look up, instead allowing Aaron to rise from his seat and acknowledge her attendance. "Hello, how may I help you?" he asked.

"Could I speak to Katrina, please," Emily asked.

Aaron walked the short distance to Katrina's desk, "Excuse me," he interrupted, knowing that Katrina was fully aware Emily was there. Katrina looked up.

"Emily, come through, it's quieter in here," Katrina gestured as she led Emily into the interrogation room. "What can I do for you today?" she asked.

"Can I trust you?" Emily naively asked.

"Trust me with what, Emily?"

"I couldn't answer your questions this morning because I don't know what my parents would do to me if they found out the truth. You saw them, they have only just started speaking to each other; it's taken a whole year for them to even talk. If I tell you the truth, can you promise me you won't tell them? They don't need to know and if you tell them it will destroy any chances of us ever being a family again."

"Emily, I can't promise that, but I will certainly take into consideration everything you tell me and discuss with you the consequences. If I feel your parents don't need to know, then yes, you have my word, but you also have to understand that I have a job to do and finding Oliver is of utmost importance. If you have anything to tell me about where he is or who broke into the room and attacked Cameron, then it's imperative you disclose that information. I want to work with you, Emily, not against you."

"It all started a few weeks ago. Oliver came back from Sydney and he said he saw someone from his past. It really upset him, his mood changed and he was clearly anxious. He wouldn't tell me who the person was or why seeing them was so upsetting for him, but he changed, he was almost paranoid. Especially when he had calls from his clients. For the first time since I had been staying with him he told them he didn't have any stock. It was as if he shut up shop to anyone calling. It was really strange; you could tell he was spooked. He even took a few days off work; he'd never taken a day off before. He said it was nothing, but I could tell it was. He never mentioned a name to me, but he started rubbing his scar more often. I remember him telling me that the scar was payback for something, but he didn't tell me what. I don't know much about his past but he did let it slip once about spending time working as a roustabout. I didn't know what that was at the time so I researched it to find it was a job in the shearing sheds. I'm not sure if that will help you to find the person responsible for Oliver's disappearance, but I feel it's connected."

"Thanks, Emily. Did Oliver have any personal papers at his house? I didn't find anything but he may have hidden them. Do you know if he had a special hiding place other than his safe?"

"No, sorry, not that I'm aware of."

"Emily, I've been told that Oliver didn't deal to any of the school crowd. Do you know if that is correct?"

"He told me that he didn't want to get involved in that market, they were too young and unstable."

"I've heard that the younger crowd is dabbling in ice, are you aware of that?"

"No, I haven't heard or seen anything like that."

"Finally, do you know of anyone else on the island dealing in drugs?"

"It's not something I go out looking for," she responded although not entirely truthfully, and prayed that Katrina wouldn't find out.

"Do you know if Oliver has a passport, I didn't find one at the house?"

"No, I'm not sure, I don't think so."

"Thank you, Emily, thanks for coming in. And no, I don't feel that your parents need to hear anything about our conversation today."

Katrina felt that she was no further ahead. If Oliver was a roustabout many years ago and this person he'd seen in Sydney was from his past, it would be almost impossible to determine where he worked. Admittedly, it would be somewhere in the outskirts of town, out in the country or even in the outback, but which Australian state was Oliver from? She had no idea; his home was devoid of any photos, any memories, any past. It was almost as if he had nothing to show from his fifty-something years. It was then she remembered Lucy. Of course, she thought, how could she have let that massive source of evidence slip through her fingers?

Five minutes later she knocked at the door. It had never occurred to her when she visited earlier in the week.

"Hello Katrina, how can I help you?" Lucy's mother, Robyn, asked.

Robyn Peyton-Smith was a wisp of a woman, the years spent battling breast cancer had most definitely taken their toll on her. Her big brown eyes still held a hidden sparkle, but overall her body's age outnumbered her years.

"I have a few questions about Oliver I hope you can help me with," Katrina said.

"You know we have been divorced for more than twenty years and I haven't laid eyes on him for that long I can't even remember," Robyn added.

"If we can go inside I have some news you may or may not want to hear, but I feel it's important to tell you regardless," Katrina said to her, hoping the response would be favourable.

"Yes, of course, come on in. What would you like, tea or coffee?" Robyn asked.

"Coffee please, white and two." Katrina watched as she made the coffee, pondering when would be the right time to break the shocking news. She wondered how much Robyn might already know, if anything.

"Robyn, have you spoken to Lucy recently?"

"No. Since she started living with the lawyer fella she hasn't been around. We aren't good enough for her new lifestyle," Robyn responded crisply.

"I may be speaking out of turn, but I feel you deserve to know what has happened. This may come as a shock to you, but Lucy is in the medical centre. She was severely attacked and raped the other night. It almost cost her her life. She's OK, but a long way from recovery. I wasn't sure if you knew or not."

"No, I haven't heard anything. Apart from the rape, is she

OK? I mean psychologically, is she going to be all right?"

"I don't know. It was very traumatic. The circumstances were unjust but profound."

"What do you mean by that?" Robyn asked.

"Lucy confided to me that her father, Oliver, raped her from when she was a ten-year-old. Are you aware of that happening?'

"She was always a very dramatic child, always wanting the limelight, always wanting to be the centre of attention. I thought it was just another of her stories. Was it true, was she telling the truth?" Robyn asked, somewhat hysterically.

"I have reason to believe so. Lucy states categorically that Oliver used to drug and rape her, that he did it until the day he moved out. She found out that Dwayne Olsen's pregnant teenage daughter, Emily, has been living with Oliver. Although Emily says she has no idea who the father of the baby is, Lucy is adamant that Oliver is the father of Emily's baby. However, Emily swears that Oliver has never touched her. The other night Lucy broke down and told her partner Troy and Dwayne Olsen about what Oliver did to her all those years ago. She told them she knew the baby would be Oliver's and that he used to drug and rape her, so chances are he was doing it to Emily as well."

"That's disgusting. Are you sure Oliver is to blame? Actually, no, forget it. Yes, that sounds about right. I always felt that something wasn't right; I just couldn't put my finger on it. I loved Oliver, he'd swept me off my feet when we first met, but he had weird sexual fantasies. I wasn't comfortable in how we made love and over time I just stopped enjoying it, and was pleased when he stopped forcing me. I must have been naïve to think that he wasn't getting it elsewhere.

"To think he was molesting my daughter, no wonder she hates me. That will be why she never bonded with her child. She didn't even want to have him. I remember her begging me to allow her an abortion, but I wouldn't listen. She had just started working at the resort and rumour was that she was an easy lay. I thought someone there had gotten her pregnant. Does Lucy think her child Peter, is Oliver's child?"

"I don't know," Katrina answered, surprised. This was news to her. She didn't even know Lucy had a child. She wondered if Lucy had disclosed that shocking piece of information to Troy.

"Will she be OK? I should go and see her. Is she still in the medical centre or is she at home?" Robyn asked.

"There is more to the story. As I mentioned, Lucy confronted Oliver and threatened to dob him into the authorities about drugging and raping her and Emily. Telling him he had to come clean, but of course he denied it."

"That sounds about right, he was always an arrogant prick. I can almost hear him refute it. Lucy would have been so infuriated. Now it all makes sense. Now I can see why they never got along."

"Robyn, Lucy was in fear for her life; she was scared he would kill her. It took her to the point of mental and physical collapse before she revealed to Troy that she'd been drugged and raped as a teenager. However, the most traumatic part of this whole experience for Lucy was telling Troy that the person who had done this to her was her father. Lucy was so ashamed she took off, firmly believing that Troy would no longer want to have anything to do with her and that his promise of marriage would never happen now that he knew the truth of who she was."

"Oh my God. That is terrible. This is all my fault. If only I had believed her, if only I had saved her from him. If only I had seen him for the bastard he was." Tears ran like a river down the crevices of her face, years of held-back tears were shed in a few moments.

Katrina wondered if she could take what was to come next,

but in order to find out about Oliver's past, she believed it necessary to push through.

"Lucy walked out of her home a few nights ago, she inadvertently walked head on into the arms of her persecutor. Oliver saw her and took the opportunity to teach her a lesson. He ferociously attacked her and finally raped her to within an inch of her life."

As Katrina spoke, she could feel each word hit its mark, like a knife stab through Robyn's heart. There was no mistaking the effect this revelation had on her. Robyn now realised who Oliver really was and what he was capable of and, if Katrina wasn't mistaken, there was something there. She sensed there was something deep inside that was screaming to come out, some hidden trauma Robyn had supressed for all these years.

"The bastard, he must pay for this! How dare he take the innocence of my daughter," Robyn fumed.

"Will you help me find him and bring him to justice?" Katrina asked.

"Yes, but how? I haven't heard from him or seen him in years, how can I help?"

"Tell me about his past, when did you meet, what was he like back then? Did he tell you anything about where he had lived, worked, who he knew or what he'd done before he came here to Clairemont Island."

No, he was a closed book. I asked him about his scar and he said it was a reminder of his sins, of a past he wanted to forget. I think he blamed his father for it. I seem to remember him saying he left home to get away from his father, but he wouldn't elaborate on that. To be honest, back then I was in love with him, so if he told me to forget about it, that's what I did, he was very persuasive. Now that I think about it, anytime I asked him about his past, he changed the conversation, and I didn't want to upset him. He had a temper, especially if he'd been drinking."

"What about drugs, what do you know of his drug habits?"

"I didn't know he took drugs, he didn't do it in front of me."

"Are you sure you can't remember anything about his past, peoples' names, places, anything that can help me piece together where he came from?"

"No, sorry. As I said, he was a closed book. I haven't been of much help, I wish there was more I could tell you. I wish I had helped Lucy when she needed it. I'm really sorry about that. He needs to be held accountable for what he's done. You can count on me to testify, anything to put the bastard away for a long time."

"There is something else that's happened." Katrina had decided only to divulge a part of the truth. "Oliver is missing. He was with a group of people when they were attacked and since then he hasn't been seen. Can you think of anywhere he might have gone to hide out. We think he might be injured and if so he may need medical attention."

Robyn was shaking her head. "No, nothing comes to mind. When we first started living together he took me to a quaint B&B in the Blue Mountains, but we never went back. I couldn't even tell you the name of the place, it wasn't anything memorable. We hardly came out of the room; we were still in that honeymoon phase, if you know what I mean. Other than that weekend, he never took me anywhere. But now that I think of it, he would stay over in Sydney, a lot. He always blamed the ferry for breaking down, but I never believed him."

"You didn't question him?" Katrina asked.

"To be honest, I let it slide to avoid an argument.

"It seems I have a lot to apologise to Lucy for. Do you think she will see me or speak to me?"

"I don't know. Perhaps ask Troy. He's a good man and truly loves her, but he'll want to protect her, so don't get your hopes up. It might be a long process, she has been deeply hurt."

"I can't think of anything else that could possibly help you," Robyn apologised.

"That's OK. I am grateful for what you have told me. And thanks for the coffee."

Katrina updated Aaron when she got back to the station. The latest news from Sean was that he was still tidying up loose ends in Sydney, trying desperately to make the last crossing of the day.

CHAPTER TWENTY-FIVE

Peace at Last

Gabby woke at 8:00 a.m. She rolled over to see that Michael had already left for his morning on the golf course; she was so exhausted she hadn't even felt him get out of bed. She opened the curtain to reveal a stream of bright sunlight. Ah, she thought, it's going to be a nice relaxed and peaceful Sunday. Days like this made her appreciate life. She was pleased that Oliver's body was found. Now Katrina would be able to put the puzzle pieces together, find the perpetrator and close the case.

Gabby dressed, had breakfast and made her way to her office in Clairemont Resort. She had a lot of paperwork to catch up on as she had, technically, been absent for most of the week. She had only just settled herself into her comfy office chair when her mobile rang; it was Scotty.

"Morning, Gabby, I just wanted to give you the heads up that Cameron will be discharged today. He's made a remarkable recovery, but as I've already told him, I don't want him to fly back to L.A. yet. Ultimately, I'd like him to stay for another week, can you make that happen?"

"Of course, he can stay another week, or longer. I will send a car for him. No actually, I'll come and pick him up myself. What time will you discharge him?" Gabby asked.

"How about 10:00 a.m.? I need to talk to him about his recovery, organise discharge meds, and I'd like him to do a few physio sessions on his shoulder."

"Do you think he will need any psychological help before he heads back to L.A.?" Gabby asked. Knowing what he had gone through; what he had experienced must have been traumatic for him.

"It wouldn't hurt, I'll ask if he wants me to organise that," Scotty responded.

"I'll come and pick him up at 10:00 a.m., see you then," Gabby advised. She felt an obligation to pick him up and show him to his new room at the resort, a room on the other side of the complex with a completely different view. She didn't want to put him in a position of reliving the past.

"Morning, Gabby. Sean arrived last night. Did you want to join us for breakfast?" Katrina asked.

"I'd love to, but I've already eaten and I need to pick Cameron up from the medical centre at 10:00 a.m. I can drop by for a coffee, or we can do lunch," Gabby suggested.

"Call by the station after you finish with Cameron. Sean is going to update Aaron and me, but that won't take long."

"Sounds like a plan," Gabby said. "See you then."

She lost herself in paperwork, her alarm reminding her to head to the medical centre. She grabbed her handbag and raced out of reception toward the resort car, passing Susan Olsen as she drove out of the resort gates. I wonder what she's doing at the resort, Gabby thought as they exchanged waves.

Joan was on front reception when Hōne entered the foyer from the west wing. "Good morning Mr Parkes, is there anything I can help you with?" she asked.

"I am waiting on the realtor you recommended, Susan Olsen. She has a few properties to show me."

"That is Susan pulling up out the front now," Joan responded.

"Thanks so much. If you are still on duty when I come back I'll tell you all about them. Apparently she has four properties to show me, but that could change as she gets an understanding of what I'm really looking for."

"That would be nice, I don't finish until 3:00 p.m.," Joan told him. There was something about him that she liked. She couldn't put a finger on it, but for some reason she felt comfortable in his presence: he had a kind face, a really cute smile and she felt he was worth getting to know. She wouldn't normally get familiar with the guests, but he seemed to be different somehow. She sensed there was an age gap between them, but that wasn't something that bothered her. Maybe just this once she would trust her gut instincts and go with the flow, and her gut intuition was definitely saying to give it a go.

She watched the way he shook Susan's hand. She noticed he held her shoulder with his other hand, she observed how he cupped the small of her back as he led her toward the entrance and then she smiled as he opened the driver's door for her, waited for her to be seated and then closed it before settling himself in the passenger seat. Joan was intrigued now; these were gestures of a gentleman, something she wasn't familiar with, especially from her past dates. Here on the island she had most definitely had her fair share of disastrous dates. Yes, of course, there had been some exceptional ones, but at thirty-five, Joan was unfortunately still single and wondered if she would ever find the right person to share the rest of her life with—she wondered if Mr Parkes could be the one.

Gabby made her way to Cameron's room. Scotty had already gone through the discharge summary with Cameron. Equipped with discharge meds, a referral to a psychologist and an appointment for physio, Cameron was flicking through a magazine as he waited for Gabby to arrive.

"Hello Cameron, you look much better than the last time I saw you. Are you ready to leave?" she asked.

"Yes, the doctor has already discharged me, I'm OK to go."

"Good, the magazine has arranged for you to stay another week, but if you don't feel up to flying I'm sure the magazine will understand if you wanted to stay longer."

"I think I'll take it one day at a time," he responded, and they drove back to the resort chatting aimlessly about the weather.

Gabby showed him to his new room at the resort and then walked to the police station. She welcomed the slight breeze of a cloudless blue sky; it was a beautiful day on Clairemont Island.

"No, the splatter marks on the roof of the boot indicate his throat was slashed inside the boot, he wasn't dumped in the boot afterwards." Sean stopped talking as Gabby entered the station.

"Sorry to interrupt," Gabby apologised.

"No problems," Katrina responded. "Sean was just finishing anyway."

"Sean, this is Gabby."

"It's nice to finally meet you; Katrina talks about you all the time," Sean responded as he rose to hug her.

"All good, I hope," Gabby smiled.

"Absolutely," Sean replied.

"She speaks highly of you, too. It's nice to finally put a face to the name," Gabby responded.

"OK, that's enough small talk. I'm dying for a coffee, shall we go?" Katrina asked.

"I reckon we are done. There isn't anything else to do apart from inform everyone that Oliver's body has been found, and I'll do that this afternoon.

Aaron and I will observe the fallout amongst the locals and try to pinpoint where they go to source a new supply of drugs. The twins will be more careful in what they do in the future, and as for Emily, well, who knows what will happen there? Maybe she will be content to stay at home and rebuild the family unit. It looked like Dwayne and Susan have started to mend some bridges, so at least something good has come out of this whole debacle.

Katrina had popped into the medical centre to see Lucy, who was still pretty heavily sedated. After discussing the seriousness of her condition and talking at great length to Troy about what this would do to their future, Lucy had concurred with Scotty's argument and agreed that he should take her to theatre later in the day to perform a hysterectomy.

Katrina apologised to Lucy, saying that she had informed her mother of everything that had happened over the last few days. Troy had not left Lucy's side and Katrina was pleased to hear that she had opened up and told Troy about her child. Troy was persuasive in convincing her that her family deserved a second chance. After all, Lucy, although not entirely to blame, had not been exactly truthful with them. Troy promised he would always have her back, would always support and protect her.

As fate would have it, Robyn called while Katrina was there, Troy answered Lucy's mobile, "Hello, you must be Troy. I am Robyn, Lucy's mum. Katrina has told me how you are looking after Lucy. I appreciate that. Is Lucy OK? I wonder if I could visit her?" she asked as Troy glanced toward Lucy, who looked as alabaster white as the hospital sheets.

"Are you up to a visit from your mum?" he asked.

"Yes, I would like that," Lucy breathed a sigh of relief. Troy could tell she genuinely meant it.

"What about Peter, can I bring him, or will that be too much for her after what has happened?" Robyn asked.

"Lucy, would you like your son to visit?" Troy asked.

"Yes, I think that's a good idea. He's not a child anymore, at fifteen he should be old enough to understand why I had nothing to do with him, why I left it to Mum to bring him up. I just pray that he forgives me. Troy, I want Mum and Peter to be part of our life now, is that OK with you?" Lucy asked.

Troy held her tightly, he looked into her bloodshot eyes, "They are your family Lucy, I want to marry you, so yes, of course they need to be part of our family from now on: it goes without saying. I'm sure that once you explain everything to Peter he will understand why you had to distance yourself from him, but you also need to apologise to your mum, she didn't know why until just now. This won't be easy for either of them. Are you sure you are ready for this right now? Why not wait until you are settled back at home after your surgery. I think that will be easier on everyone. It will give you a chance to heal and give them a bit of time to get over this shocking revelation."

"Can Mum hear me?" Lucy asked.

Troy handed over the mobile to Lucy. "Mum, yes, we would love to have you both come and visit us once I'm back home, but if you wanted to come and see me after my surgery, I'd love that."

"I'd love that, too. Ask Troy to call me when you are out of surgery and I'll pop over. When is your surgery?" she asked.

"In a couple of hours," Lucy responded.

"I'll be thinking of you," Robyn said as she hung up. She had already decided to tell Peter everything when he came home from school. She wanted him to have digested the information and hoped that she could answer all his questions before she took him over to see his mother.

Katrina left the hospital and walked the short distance to the police station.

Back at the police station, everything hinged now on finding the Asian man.

"I'm confident he is the driver of the Audi. I'm certain now that he is the one who topped Oliver. But was the driver acting alone? Is he the person who Oliver saw in Sydney? Is he the person from his past?" Katrina added as she scrunched her shoulders with the tension.

"I suppose we will have to wait and see, but at least we can rest knowing that Oliver is not going to drug and rape anyone else. Lucy and Emily can move ahead with their lives knowing he can't harm them any more than he already has," Katrina said firmly.

The four chatted amongst themselves as Katrina led them down the promenade to her favourite café. "Wow, what an incredible view," Sean said as he stopped to take a good long look at the lighthouse, beach and surrounding vista of Clairemont Island. "It was too dark last night when I arrived to appreciate the view."

"That's why I always tell you I'm living in a beautiful piece of paradise; now do you believe me?" Katrina proudly acknowledged. "I'll be surprised if you want to go back to Sydney after spending a week here," She winked at Gabby, knowing the island had captured the heart of many of its visitors. Would Sean be the next victim?

"You don't read Gatsby," I said.

"To learn whether adultery is good or bad but to learn about how complicated issues such as adultery and fidelity and marriage are.

A great novel heightens your senses and sensitivity to the complexities of life and of individuals, and prevents you from self-righteousness that sees morality in fixed formulas about good and evil."
Azar Nafisi

Trust The Universe

In *Trust the Universe* Vicki reveals how she dismissed intuition, gut instincts and messages 'from above' as she believed the messages she was receiving were so far-fetched they couldn't possibly be true.

But the Universe had its own plan for her and kept opening doors and connecting her to people of influence, until the 'slap in the face' the Universe was giving her could no longer be ignored.

What happened next became a catalyst for change; one by one circumstances occurred that would ultimately bring about an unbelievable outcome.

This book takes you on a personal journey and is just one example of what is possible when you let go of fear-based practices; when you believe in yourself and *Trust the Universe*.

Memory Of Your Life

Memory of Your Life is a step-by-step workbook designed to share your life stories with loved ones.

This simple, easy-to-use workbook gently guides you through life's most important memories and helps you record and share them in fine detail with poise, passion and purpose. It gives you opportunity to write anything left unsaid and give insights into the real you.

When Vicki began showing people this step-by-step workbook concept it became evident that many people resonated with it, they felt the same way, and it identified the need for a platform, like this workbook, to encourage people to record their stories and share them with family and friends.

Deadly Deception

Deadly Deception came about quite by chance; an avid fan of crime stories herself, Vicki embarked on a journey of mystery, revealing she didn't even know who did it until she wrote the words. She describes the writing process by saying that once she got 'out of the way' the characters took over and revealed their individual involvement in the crime.

The story is set on Clairemont Island, a secluded island in the South Pacific. Breathtakingly beautiful this island has many a story to tell. The lies, deceit and secrets of the residents and holidaymakers will make your hair curl.

When a crime is committed, it's up to the residents to race against time to uncover the murderer before a cyclone hits the island and potentially destroys all evidence.

Nobody is beyond suspicion.

About the Author

New Zealand born Vicki Williams lives in Australia. Vicki has always had a passion to write, but lacked the confidence to do anything more with her stories. That was until she entered a challenge to write a book in forty hours and shocked herself by producing her first book *Trust the Universe*.

Vicki has successfully taken other authors from story conception to publication as she mentors and teaches 'How to Write' workshops in person and online.

Vicki continues writing the Clairemont Island mystery series, as well as a young adult series written under the pen name of Jade Green. With a drawer full of possible storylines, it will be interesting to see where she leads us in the future.

vickiwilliamsauthor.com.au

www.ingramcontent.com/pod-product-compliance
Lightning Source LLC
Chambersburg PA
CBHW032003130726
47903CB00012B/743